BLOOD
VENGEANCE

P. A. DUNCAN

DEDICATION

To all those who battle injustice, overtly and covertly, and bring war criminals to justice.

CONTENTS

ACKNOWLEDGEMENTS

My thanks to friends, neighbors, teachers, professors, former students, and co-workers for their support and encouragement. My gratitude to the love of my life for his patience and belief in me.

To the above acknowledgements, I'd like to add all my writer friends in SWAG Writers and Shenandoah Valley Writers for their encouragement, too, and for challenging me to do better.

EPIGRAPH

"A father's no shield for his child."

Seamus Heaney, "Elegy"

GIVING THE DEAD BACK THEIR NAMES

July 1995
The Amsterdam Hilton

A check of his watch told Alexei Bukharin his wife had been in the shower for forty-five minutes. Before he could decide whether to go remind her he got a turn, too, his nephew, Kolya, emerged from the second bedroom of the suite. Clad only in a towel around his waist, Kolya made directly for the room service Alexei had ordered.

Kolya wrinkled his nose as he passed his uncle. "*Dyadya*, you still stink." Then, he dug into the meats and cheeses with abandon.

For more than a week, the three of them had been hostages along with Dutch Peacekeepers, held by the Serbs inside a U.N. base near Srebrenica. Hundreds of women and girls had been left there with them, after a Serbian paramilitary unit took the men and boys. Trying to feed them all with a small supply of MREs had proved trying. After some tense negotiations, they and the Dutch soldiers had been evacuated to Amsterdam. The Muslim women and girls were left to the international relief workers.

"This is wonderful, *Dyadya*," Kolya said around a mouthful. "All I want to do for the next week is eat and sleep. Where is *Tetya*?"

"My wife is indulging in one of her hour-long showers," Alexei said.

Kolya stopped pouring a glass of vodka and looked up, his face showing some emotion.

"What?"

Kolya's mask came up. He finished pouring the vodka and shrugged. "Nothing."

Alexei pitched his voice to command level. "Tell me."

Kolya downed half the vodka in one gulp. "It matters nothing now."

1

Alexei switched to Russian. "*Rasskazhi mne.*" Tell me.

Kolya shrugged again. "I don't think she should be left alone."

Alexei moved at once to the pile of clothing she had discarded. Stiff from sweat and dirt, they were heavy as he picked through them. Her guns were there, both of them, as were the two commando knives she carried.

He turned back to his nephew. "What happened?'

"I wasn't going to tell you."

"But now you are."

Between shoving food in his mouth, Kolya explained. "That night she and I went to reconnoiter, we went to a soccer stadium, crept up to the loading docks, and made our way inside through the ducting. The Serbs had put four, five thousand men and boys on the playing field. We could hear them asking for food and water they'd been promised."

Kolya downed more vodka. "Then, the Serbs opened up on them. The shooting went on for a long time. She took pictures. When the Serbs walked among the bodies giving the coup de grace, I had to stop her from going down to the field. So, we left. As we made our way back to the U.N. base, we came across a group of *Chetniks*, at least they were dressed in Serb camouflage. They were about to rape a girl, no more than twelve. I fired into the air and they ran, but *Tetya*... She shot the one closest to her because he raised a gun. When she checked to make sure he was dead she saw he was no older than the girl."

"Shit!" Alexei headed for the bathroom.

Mai Fisher was a shadow, insubstantial, behind the frosted glass of the shower doors. He could see her moving in the spray of water, but he glanced around the bathroom for anything she could hurt herself with. He saw nothing. He sat on the lowered top of the toilet and began to unlace his boots. He'd waited long enough for the shower. Eye level with the vanity, he noticed a round mirror there with a sprinkling of a white powder on it. Dampening a finger on his tongue, he blotted the powder, and brought the finger back to his mouth. Cocaine.

Alexei stripped off his filthy clothing and entered the large, marble shower stall.

Mai stood against a corner, her back to the marble as the topmost jet from the shower tower sprayed her with a strong blast of hot water. Alexei saw nothing more serious than a bruise or a scrape, but her eyes were closed. One hand held her hair off her face.

Alexei stepped into the spray and let it wash over him. Her eyes opened and wandered over his body. He had more than scrapes and bruises. New scars, a lot of them, were bright against his pale skin. Her eyes came up to his, and she smiled, though she was somewhere far away.

"What took you so long?" she asked. "I was waiting, thinking it's been a long time since we fucked standing up."

Without waiting for his consent—as if she needed it—she reached for him, her hands stroking, her mouth on his, as the water cascaded.

Alexei took her by the shoulders and pulled her away. "Where did you get the cocaine?"

She didn't protest his knowing and shrugged. "Most of my teen years I spent partying in Amsterdam. The drugs may have changed, but the sources are the same."

"Why?"

"Because I can't look at the faces anymore. The faces in my head. There are too many of them."

Alexei embraced her, holding her head beneath his chin. The faces in his head she had helped him dispel, but he knew he couldn't offer the same to her. She wouldn't have it.

When someone finally counted the dead of Srebrenica, Alexei doubted there'd be enough cocaine on earth to get her through it. He could justify killing what looked like a Serb in an army uniform to stop rape. Mai would only see a child she killed. She would see herself no better than the killers and rapists of children.

He leaned down so his lips were close to her ear. "You promised me about the cocaine."

"Let's not make a big deal of it. It was once and not that much. I'm more upset that the effects are so transitory."

"This was too soon, all this death. Too soon after Kansas City. I should have said no when we were sent here."

Her arms at last embraced him. "That's not the issue. I was ready."

"I wasn't. Fuck this job. We're leaving here and going home, and we're taking a year off, maybe the rest of our lives off. I won't lose you to this madness. Do you hear me?"

"I'm all right." She tipped her head back, and he saw her smile before her mouth found his. When she broke the kiss, her laugh was low and warm. "I still want to fuck." She pressed her body against him. "And so do you."

"I don't fuck my wife. I love her."

"Let's debate semantics later."

The kissing didn't stop, nor did his thoughts. The debates were always later, but debating the killing of children was a topic he would avoid.

* * *

May 1997
Near Bratunac, Serbia

The tour of the killing field was brief. What interested the forensic scientist more than the place of death were the recovered bodies. Where they died was secondary to why he was here: to restore the names taken from them in hasty death. That was his mission, and he wanted to be about it. He cut the interpreter off in mid-sentence and asked to be taken to the tent erected as a temporary morgue. Though the U.N. worker seemed distracted by the change in plans, he obligingly led the way.

The group side-stepped down a steep hill, slippery from Spring rains, and reached a small valley flat enough for the large, white tent that was the morgue. The tent itself was a long slash on the valley floor, leaving barely enough room for trucks and other equipment. U.N. Peacekeepers in blue berets ringed the tent, their weapons at the ready. The scientist wondered why the dead had to be guarded but remembered there were some who wouldn't want the dead to have their names.

The forensic scientist was a retired aviation accident investigator, renowned for his ability to identify remains in the worst possible condition. With a bit of flesh from an accident site and a DNA sample from a relative, he could provide a family with something to bury. Even before DNA sequencing made some of his job easier, he had pioneered facial reconstruction techniques for forensic identification. At the time, his work had been revolutionary. For most of the history of plane crashes, unidentifiable remains were buried in a single grave, sometimes in a single coffin.

At first, people found it incredible he didn't need whole bodies to make an identification, that a scrap of bone could reveal gender, age, medical, or injury history to his trained eye. Because of his genius and his dedication to solving problems, many a full-sized casket went into the ground with only a hank of skin and bone. A name and date of death for a specific person could go on a marker. That mattered to loved ones left behind. The only drawback was the number of casualties in an airplane crash kept him occupied for months.

He was optimistic about this job for the U.N. Identifying victims of a massacre should be child's play compared to the jigsaw puzzle of plane crash casualties. That he could bring closure to people, he was confident as he walked toward the tent. And it was a good addition to his resume. His pension was more than adequate, but there was no reason why he shouldn't take advantage of his unique skills. This might be a big enough job he could raise his consulting fees.

When he reached the tent, he felt his confidence buoy. There were massive, portable air conditioning units pumping cold air into the structure. That meant someone knew what was needed to be done to make his work efficient. He could feel the cold air leaking from the tent and realized it would be costing a pretty penny to keep this up. And that was good. No government bean-counting here.

A soldier at the tent's opening—a Finn by the embroidered flag on his uniform—checked everyone's identification and passes, then held the tent flap aside for them to enter. The scientist was unfazed when the smells billowed from the opening.

Dank, moldy earth, and corruption past the cloyingly sweet state he was most familiar with at accident sites. He heard several of his staff gag, but he knew to breathe through his mouth. He took a small jar of Vicks VapoRub from a pocket and put a generous amount on his upper lip, atop his graying mustache. His staff passed the jar around until the biting smell of Vicks overcame everything else. The soldier smiled with some condescension. He'd been here long enough to become inured.

The scientist re-pocketed the small, blue jar, and removed his hat, exposing his bald head to the weak sun. He stepped forward, into the tent and to the side to give room for his staff.

"Jesus Christ! someone said.

The tent covered row on row of tables, some manufactured, some makeshift. Sheets of white plastic covered each table, and atop the plastic were lumps of indistinguishable meat, an occasional skull, a femur, an ulna, a rib protruding from rotted cloth.

He hadn't been told this. These bodies and body parts had been buried for months, perhaps years. From a quick assessment he could see mounds of decaying flesh with multiple heads and too many arms. Decomposition had congealed the remains. This was madness.

"Who is in charge here?" he demanded.

From a corner of the tent a woman walked forward, a white lab coat over black BDUs. Her hands were inside latex gloves, and a bio-hazard mask covered the lower half of her face. Except for two white streaks at her temples, her hair was dark, as were her eyes, and when she spoke, it was with a cultured, English accent.

"I suppose I am. I'm Mai Fisher from the U.N. You must be Dr. Clifton Hume." Her latex gloves were dark with dirt and something else, and she didn't offer a hand to shake.

"Yes, I am. This..." Hume waved a hand toward some nearby remains, barely recognizable as human. "This isn't what I expected."

Fisher removed her mask, and Hume saw she was in her thirties. Good skin. She had the typical round skull of those of Celtic descent.

"This is Bosnia, Doctor," she said. "What did you expect?"

Hume was unaccustomed to such sarcasm. "How long have these people been in the ground?"

"Two years."

Hume heard his staff muttering in disbelief, but he began to understand the challenge. He knew he wouldn't walk away from it. "Any idea how many?"

"Here? A hundred or so. Stored in the caves nearby, probably 7,000-plus."

"Oh my God," one of his staff said.

Fisher didn't react to the interruption. "They are Bosnian Muslim males between the ages of sixteen and eighty. They were shot at four to five different locations in and around the safe area of Srebrenica in July 1995. The bodies were bulldozed into mass graves. We have a list of missing men compiled by the women who survived, along with identifying information. In many cases there will be family for DNA comparisons. On occasion we find an identity card, but that's rare. They were robbed before they were murdered."

"This could take us years."

"My understanding is that you're retired and have time on your hands. The U.N. War Crimes Tribunal has allocated sufficient funds to see this to the end, and your contract will be extended as necessary."

Hume glanced around again. As both a scientist and a humanist, this project was more than tempting: to put families at ease, give them something to bury in a place where they could mourn.

Yet, the extent of the tragedy was almost overwhelming. Seven thousand lives ended, their mortal remains scraped under the earth like so much unwanted debris.

"Why did this happen?" he asked Mai Fisher.

Her expression made him feel foolish, as if he'd asked not a rhetorical question, but an unanswerable one.

She shrugged and replied, "Who knows? Maybe the fathers and grandfathers of these men were in the *Utashi* in World War II and killed *Chetniks*, and now the *Chetniks* got revenge. Maybe it goes back to the Battle of Kosovo in 1689. Maybe it's as simple as madmen out of control, or young soldiers with a blood lust thinking they're settling ancient scores. No one can ever really know why, but no one really cares, either. This is only Bosnia."

Hume considered her words. The quiet in the tent lured him to watch some of the U.N. workers moving about, making notes or taking care in covering the remains with something that could only be reverence. He looked at the woman before him, whose eyes were so devoid of humanity.

"You care," he said.

She didn't respond but something in her eyes shifted, and he thought he saw her gratitude.

Once again he looked over what was to become his domain for the next few years. What lay before him was an opportunity of a lifetime.

In his years of forensic identification at aircraft accidents all over the world, he'd identified perhaps two or three thousand bodies. Maybe more. He'd stopped counting a long time ago.

In this one place he could double that experience and, more importantly, advance forensic science well into the next century. Yet, the scope was staggering, even for a young man—and he was not that anymore—but the stark humanity of this effort and the burden borne by this young woman was compelling.

Fisher broke into his reverie. "We've arranged for shelter for you and your staff a few miles away at the U.N. compound. The prefabs are more crude than the usual hotel but more comfortable than any hotel around here. After every four days, you'll get three off. There'll be transport to Zagreb, Vienna, Rome."

"You seem to think this is a fait accompli," Hume told her.

She gave him a slight smile, and he saw a broader one would make her more attractive than she appeared. "If you don't do this, the take on you was all wrong."

"The take on me?"

"Your former colleagues at the FAA assured me you particularly enjoy a challenge."

"Challenges, yes. Impossibilities?" Hume looked around again, surprised the scene wasn't yet seared in his brain. "Are you absolutely certain about the number?" She nodded. "Look, sometimes relatives exaggerate. Sometimes they try to defraud, especially if a government is involved. One plane crash I did in Africa, the government offered $300 per victim to the families. If all the families who came forward claiming a relative on board, there would have been about a thousand people on that 737."

"I'm certain. This was a military operation."

"Sometimes militaries, as we know in America, up the body-count for propaganda effect."

"In this case, if anything, the military down-played the body count, Dr. Hume. The range I gave you is accurate. It has been verified independently, and there is a likelihood we'll find more mass graves."

"How can you be so certain?"

At first Hume thought she wouldn't answer, and he was startled by the expression on her face. He had triggered the memory of some horror she had buried, likely the same time these bodies went into the ground. When she did reply, he had to strain to hear, but he understood. That secured his resolve to stay and work.

"I was there."

* * *

May 1997
U.N. Compound, Bratunac, Serbia

Sometimes Mai Fisher felt like Lady MacBeth, bemoaning the gouts of blood only she could see on her hands and which never paled after constant washing. When she pulled off the filthy latex gloves at the end of each day, she still felt as if the stench and mess of death had been tattooed into her skin. She wished emotions could be as easily discarded as latex gloves and white lab coats—packed up and sent away for biomedical disposal.

No, emotions followed her everywhere, especially when she tried to cast them off. They crowded into her thoughts, her dreams, her sleep, what she could manage of that. Perhaps now that Clifton Hume had arrived, she would leave. Distance would lessen her guilt, and there would be sleep. Maybe then the faces that haunted her dreams would go back to their own hell and wait until this cruel land called her back, as she knew it would.

She returned again and again because, unable to stop massacres, she atoned by surrounding herself with the victims, starting with the project to identify the remains from Srebrenica. That was beyond her skills, and she did her part by selecting the person she knew could do what she couldn't.

When she had read his scientific works one item stood out for her. Hume likened forensic identification to restoring the lost names of the dead. Mai's solace came in knowing the women of Srebrenica would have a place to go to and mourn their husbands and sons and fathers.

The men of Srebrenica would have their names back, but their souls would forever be restless in Mai's conscience.

Twenty years ago in the midst of the Cold War, she had become a spy, more from family legacy than anything. The Cold War had been black and white, good and evil, two sides she could define with ease. Its aftermath was a gray area where friends became enemies and enemies friends, and her long-established methods were often insufficient for a new era.

Successes had come easy in the Cold War, and failure was too common in its passing. Her ideals were outmoded, her optimism naïve. Though her skills were unsurpassed, the world of hands-on spying had devolved into ubiquitous, privacy-intruding cameras, satellites, and electronic eavesdropping. She suspected someone, somewhere would end up short for taking the human factor out of espionage.

The Balkans. Africa. The Middle East. China. Korea. India. Pakistan. Northern Ireland. So many global hotspots, so few spies who could infiltrate or suborn. Yet, why put people at risk when you had satellites in orbit that could read newspaper headlines over your shoulder or parabolic microphones that picked up conversations from their vibrations on windows?

And part of her had grown tired of it. That was the biggest shock of all. She had never envisioned a day when the intrigue, risk, and danger wouldn't lure her, but that day fast approached.

Hume's innocent question about how she could be so certain at the number of victims had rattled her. She had realized how futile her work had become. She had been there, seen most of it, and was able to stop none of it.

Mai shook her head to clear it of the thoughts that made the butt of her gun fit too neatly into her hand, press too quickly against her temple. She was one person who could not stop armies bent on ethnic cleansing, and she needed to understand that. She should; she was half-Irish.

No, she would be at peace tonight, knowing Dr. Hume's work would lay the ghosts of Srebrenica to rest and return the dead their names.

Except for the constant companion of her waking and sleeping hours—one boy, dressed like a soldier, who lay alone and unnamed in a grave no one would ever find.

CAREER DAY

N atalia Bukharin waited in the kitchen for her grandparents to emerge from their office. They would know she was home from school because it was the usual time and because the house's elaborate security system would have heralded her arrival.

She poured herself some orange juice and sat at the counter, her eyes not leaving the closed office door. Two lights on the keypad glowed, one green to indicate they were in there behind a locked door, one red to indicate they could not be disturbed.

That had been one of the cardinal rules—obey the lights. Don't go into the office until one or the other was with her. Don't knock on the door when the red light was on unless it was an emergency—"a life-and-death emergency, not a I-need-a-new-dress emergency" had been her step-grandmother's definition.

There had been another cardinal rule when she was younger—don't enter the grandparents' bedroom unless you knocked first. That rule had been put in place when she was eight years old and had just come to live with them. One night after waking from a particularly bad nightmare where her mother died over and over again in that car wreck, she pushed open the door to their room.

So, she'd seen them having sex. She'd been eight after all and was well aware what adults sometimes did behind closed doors. Then, she'd decided it was pretty gross and didn't see why adults went through all the fuss. Older now, she had begun to understand the allure of sex.

Natalia smiled when she remembered Mai's reaction to her coy question about why she had to knock—a lot of big words Natalia knew boiled down to "don't come in because we're having sex." But Natalia was almost eighteen now, and the nightmares about her mother's death were well behind her. Her adolescence made her reject the need to seek her grandparents out in the middle of the night.

Of course, the closed and locked office door didn't necessarily mean they were working. It could mean they had started out working and then had sex. They had sex a lot—she could tell from the glances, the shared laughter, the way her grandfather would touch Mai's hand or face. At this age everything for Natalia was tainted with sex, and though the thought of her grandparents indulging in it was unnerving, it was also exciting and mysterious.

Right now, that was irking her because she needed to talk to them about stupid school stuff. In truth she thought her grandfather's and step-grandmother's relationship was pretty amazing, especially because they wanted to do the wild thing so often after so long being together. She wondered if it was her grandfather's insecurity. He was fifteen years older than his wife, and Natalia supposed that meant something entirely different when he was thirty-five and Mai was twenty than now that he was nearly sixty and joked about trophy husbands.

Marrying a much younger person for a second marriage go-round seemed to run in the family. Her new stepmother was also more than a decade younger than her father. Natalia hoped that boded well for her when she was in her forties.

Mai would laugh at that, but her grandfather Alexei would get all stern and say, "Natalia, you are much too young to think of such things." Her stepmother would give a nervous smile that meant she thought it was a plot against her. Her father, being her father, would freak.

Natalia checked the clock in the kitchen. She'd been home from school for almost a half hour, so the fact her grandparents hadn't emerged from the office right away meant she was right about what they were doing in there. The annoyance flared again because they weren't operating on her schedule, something Mai would call "adolescent arrogance." At school when kids bitched about their parents, Natalia would chime in, but inside she had always considered them wise and totally cool.

She began to tap her fingers on the counter. Really, how long did it take? She had no idea of course. In her fantasies about a particular boy at school, it lasted for hours. He was definitely daydream-worthy, the kind where naked bodies pressed together and there were multiple orgasms.

Natalia smiled at the reaction she might get if she were to ask Mai, "What does an orgasm feel like?"

Since that had nothing to do with what she wanted to discuss, she filed it away for the perfect, future use. The times when she saw Mai nonplussed were rare, but Natalia had managed on occasion to render her speechless. Being a teenager sucked most of the time, really, but there were the rare occasions when you put one over on the adults, and you knew there was nothing they could do about it.

Okay, they know I want to talk to them, so they're doing this on purpose.

The two lights on the keypad went out, indicating the door was no longer locked. She waited a moment, breath held, and the door opened. They entered the family room amid Mai's throaty laughter and her grandfather whispering into her ear. Their faces were flushed, and, oh yes, Mai's hair was slightly mussed. Christ, they had been at it again. Sometimes Natalia thought they waited for her to be out of the house so they could jump each other on every piece of furniture.

"Hello, Mums, Popi," Natalia greeted.

"Were you waiting?" Mai asked.

Well, duh.

"How was school?" her grandfather asked.

"The same as yesterday," Natalia said.

"Was yesterday boring or unfulfilling? I can't remember which," he teased.

Natalia rolled her eyes in the quintessential adolescent gesture, but she adored her grandfather, Alexei Bukharin. He was tall and handsome for an old guy and wore his hair longer than most grandfathers. It was nearly all gray, but it was totally cool. He had always been fun to be with and gave comfort whenever she needed it, whether she knew she needed it or not. He had taught her things she would never learn in decades of school—how to hammer nails and build decks, put up drywall, navigate a motorboat, and sail. She knew he would always be there, which was certainly more than she could say for her own father, who had dumped her on her grandparents when she was eight.

That was unfair to Daddy. Her father had been critically injured in the same accident that killed her mother. Natalia had escaped without a scratch, and her father had found that difficult to deal with. No questions asked, her grandparents had taken her in, and she had a decent adjustment.

Natalia knew Mai loved her, but she also had a boatload of expectations. Theirs was sometimes the contentious relationship between mother and daughter, but that had only come about with what Mai called the "raging hormones" of Natalia's teenaged years. Even when Mai was right, Natalia was compelled to be rebellious. And Mai was nothing if not omniscient. Natalia had no secrets to call her own. Mai wasn't a snoop; she could look at you, and you spilled your guts.

Like right now. Mai studied Natalia with a practiced eye. "What's up at school?" she asked.

"Oh, it's nothing really."

Natalia gave her best long-suffering sigh. If she could milk the sympathy thing a little, she might get an hour added to her weekend curfew.

Her grandfather's face molded into concern for her, but Mai showed her skepticism. Since Popi was the sympathetic one, she addressed him.

"We have, like, this totally stupid, bogus assignment, and I'm letting you know I'm, like, going to blow it off."

"What is it?" he asked.

"I told you. It's really stupid. It's not important enough to bother you with."

Mai spoke as she walked past her to the refrigerator. "Obviously, it's something or you wouldn't have brought it up."

Mai poured herself a glass of cranberry juice then leaned on the counter across from Natalia and stared.

I really, really hate it when she's right, which is, like, all the time, Natalia thought.

"Look, it's dumb, and, besides, I can't do it anyway."

Her grandfather came close and laid a hand on her shoulder. "*Dedushka*, you can do anything you put your mind to."

"No, it's not that I'm not capable. It's, like, I can't."

Now the two of them stared at her as if she'd grown an extra nose or something.

"Okay, well, we're having, like, this stupid Career Day thing at school in a couple of weeks, and all of us had to, like, write down what our parents did, and, so, like, I put down my Dad was an astronomer, and the stupid teacher goes, 'Well, Natalia, your father isn't here to be a guest at career day, so write down what your grandfather does,' and I said, 'This is the 20th century. My grandmother works, too,' and she said, well add that, and so that's, like, why I can't."

The two of them still stared at her. Natalia had expected panic, not this blandness.

"What did you tell her we do?" her grandfather asked.

"I said, 'They work for the U.N.,' which was, like, totally not good because then, like, she wanted to know all about it, and, like, I had to say, 'I don't know,' because I don't know, and she's, like, 'You don't know what they do?' and I'm, like, 'No, I don't,' and she goes, 'Well, you have to know something,' and I go, 'Like, no, I don't.'"

Natalia paused for a breath.

Mai shook her head and didn't hide her laugh. "Amazing. That was all one sentence. Thank God you're more articulate when you write."

"What's the bottom line?"

That was her grandfather. Straight to the point. Mai liked to let you twist in the wind a bit.

"I tried to tell her you were too busy to come to Career Day, and she said, 'Lots of parents are busy, but they make time for something like this, so have your grandparents call me.'"

"All right, we'll call her and give her our regrets," he said. "Which teacher is it?"

Natalia looked first at Popi then at Mai and summoned her resolve.

"What exactly do you do, anyway?"

"We work for the United Nations," her grandfather said.

"Well, duh, Popi, so do, like, thousands of other people. What do you do?"

This time her grandparents did exchange a look, one Natalia had often seen, and it somehow spoke volumes.

"You had to know I was going to ask some day. I mean, all these strange people come and go, like Uncle Snake—I mean, who has an honorary uncle named Snake? And there's my Russian cousin Kolya who has that weird skull tattoo, and Olga, my 'au pair' who acts like everyone who comes near me is going to kidnap me or something. The two of you go away a lot, sometimes weeks at a time, and I never know when you're coming back. So, I think you're like…"

"Like what?" Mai demanded. That was the tone—demanding.

"I don't know. The Mafia or something."

Mai tried to stifle a laugh, but Popi was serious. "No, we're not in the Mafia, American, Italian, or Russian. We…"

"What?"

"Well, we advise governments on security matters. That means our work is classified, so we won't be able to participate in your Career Day."

She hated it when he was right, too. "I mean, couldn't Mai come and talk about EuroEnterprises. You said it was totally cool to talk about being an intern over the summer and going to Bosnia."

"How important is this to you?" Mai asked.

"Well, I'll be, like, the only one without parents or steps or anything coming. I mean, if you sent Roisin O'Said, it won't be the same."

"Why would I send Roisin?"

"Well, she's, like your COO or something, right?"

"Yes, but I'm the CEO."

"Which is fine," Alexei said. "So long as you don't decide you need a trophy husband."

"Can a trophy wife have a trophy husband?" Mai teased back.

Natalia gave another of her sighs. They could joke at the bloody stupidest times.

"Well?"

Mai smiled at her. "I'll be happy to come."

Natalia nodded, but there were still too many unanswered questions.

"Why do I think this conversation isn't over?" Mai asked.

"I really, really would like to know exactly what it is you do. Like, why Popi nearly got killed in Kansas City that time, like why I came into the bathroom once and found you bleeding, Mai? Sometimes I see cuts and bruises on you both, so why…"

"I think we got the picture," Alexei said.

For a second Natalia thought she'd angered her grandfather, but she saw his expression was full of regret.

"It's not something we can discuss with you, for your safety. It's why we keep a low profile and why Olga is your bodyguard."

"I don't understand."

"Let's say there are people in the world who don't abide by their laws or the regulations of the U.N., which they swore to do. We make certain their governments know about their actions. As you might imagine, that can make these people unhappy, so they try to stop us from turning them in."

Natalia mulled that and nodded. "So, you're like spies."

"Why would you think that?" Mai asked.

Sometimes they equated youth with being totally dense.

"Well, for starters, Dad told me that Popi and Uncle Snake got him out of Russia. That's not exactly a normal thing for someone to do. Then, there's Olga, who knows all of these really odd things…"

Mai interrupted her. "I doubt very seriously Olga has discussed odd things with you."

"No, but sometimes she says things like, 'Little One, if you see same car follow us more than three turns, tell me right away.'" Natalia thought her imitation of Olga's thick Russian accent was pretty decent. "So, how does she know things like that?"

Alexei crossed his arms over his chest. "I think you've been watching too many movies."

"Okay, look, I can see this, like, makes you guys uncomfortable, but don't treat me as if I'm stupid. It's not because I watch too much TV or too many movies. It's because fucking weird things go on here."

Popi looked at Mai, exasperation in his tone. "It's because of you that she so fluidly interjects the word fucking into her speech."

"Why would I think she listens to that when she doesn't listen to anything else I say?" Mai replied.

Natalia stood up. "Look, we are not getting side-tracked into one of your little joke fests. I'm right, aren't I?"

Mai came from around the counter and faced her. "And what if you were? Do you think that means we could come to Career Day and talk about it?"

"Oh, please. That is so not the point."

"Then, what is?"

"I would like to know the truth."

Natalia sensed her grandfather at her side, and she hadn't seen him move.

"Do you think we've lied to you?" he asked her.

"Well, no, not exactly lied. You know, like the President once said—depends on what is, is."

"I hardly think you can compare my integrity to his."

His face was so serious, Natalia realized she had to lighten things up. "Well, you do have the same color hair."

That didn't mollify him. He turned a wounded look on Mai. "Some help would be appreciated," he said.

"Your hair is the same color but much nicer," she replied.

"Guys, no joke fest, remember," Natalia said.

Mai's gaze was far less forgiving than Popi's. "If you think we've lied to you, I'd like some specifics."

Of course, she would ask that, knowing full well Natalia was operating on impressions, feelings, and a teenager's self-centeredness.

"Well, you always say you're away on business."

"When we're away, we are on business."

Stupid question that was. "Okay, then, like I said, who has an honorary uncle named Snake who sees people stalking him behind every tree and shrub?"

Mai shrugged. "That's it?"

"He said he used to be in the CIA."

"A lot of people work at the CIA in many different capacities."

Natalia knew Mai would have answers, but, really, she didn't have to give them.

"I saw him once before he put a jacket on, and he wears a gun."

Mai lifted an eyebrow. "This is America. A lot of people carry guns."

"So do you."

"We've explained this to you," Mai said. "We own guns…"

"No. You wear one. Almost all the time. I mean, it's not, like, out there, but I've seen it." She looked at her grandfather. "You, too."

"So, we wear the guns we own," Mai said. "Popi explained about people getting upset with us because we uncover their crimes."

"How do you do that, prove people have committed crimes?"

"We either catch them in the act, or we find proof of it."

"How?"

Mai looked to Alexei. "I could use some help myself."

"Your hair looks nothing like the President's," he said.

Natalia caught the icy look Mai gave him, but when Mai turned to her, her face was blank.

"If you think we've lied to you, you need to understand, that is, try to rationalize, that at times dishonesty can protect you. You have to take our word for it."

That was reasonable, Natalia knew. She didn't feel like being reasonable.

"That time I found you bleeding in the bathroom—what happened? And not, 'I got mugged,' like you told me at the time."

"This conversation is over!"

Natalia almost jumped at the anger in her grandfather's voice. "Popi…"

"No, it's over. Mai will come to Career Day as part of EuroEnterprises. There will be no more talk about spies. Am I clear?"

She felt her face flush. The times her grandfather had raised his voice were, well—she couldn't remember when he'd ever done it before. That brought her temper to the fore.

"Fine! I guess if I'm that untrustworthy, I'll go to my room."

"I don't respond to a child's guilt trips," he said.

"Well, then, I'll just, like, accept the fact that both of you have lied to me, like, my entire fucking life!"

She whirled and stomped from the room, and made sure they could hear each stair she trod.

* * *

Mai Fisher turned to her husband and said, "Oh, yes, the Neanderthal approach really works."

"What else could I do? Tell her we're spies?"

"I think she's figured that out."

He studied her face, capable of reading so much. "Surely you don't want to start answering her questions? If you do, you'll have to tell her you were shot that time she found you. After that, you know what the next question would be."

Mai could read him, too. "She'd want to know if you or I had ever shot anyone."

"Precisely why I opted for the Neanderthal approach."

"We're well past the time where she accepts the first thing we can think of to tell her. She's smart, too smart for her own good right now. She's spotted our guns. How long before she sees through the whole subterfuge?"

"A subterfuge which, for spies, we haven't done a good job of maintaining."

"Obviously we've been complacent, and just as obviously, Olga hasn't been circumspect."

Alexei shrugged and gave Mai a smile. "Maybe Olga thinks she's still recruiting for the KGB."

"Not funny."

"I'm sure Olga has only told her what's necessary for her personal security."

Mai looked away, thinking, considering, but what she said surprised him. "If we tell her she can't talk about this, she won't."

"I don't want to put her in that situation. Look, I understand the older she gets, the likelihood she picks up on more of this is high, and that means the possibility of her becoming a target grows as well. And Olga isn't getting any younger. In fact, she's three years older than I."

"I didn't notice your age about a half hour ago."

"Much can be achieved in skillful hands."

"Yes, well, that aside, she isn't going to let this go."

His face became an inflexible mask. "We are not telling my granddaughter anything about what we really do. That's final."

* * *

Much like his granddaughter, he turned on his heel and strode back into the office, locking the door behind him. Mai could excuse Natalia for walking off in a huff. You expected that of a teenager. The same behavior from a man in his fifties wasn't acceptable.

Which to deal with first? She drained her cranberry juice, wished it were whiskey, and headed upstairs.

"I'm on the computer," came the muffled reply when Mai knocked on Natalia's door. Mai rapped harder and could almost hear the pained sigh from the other side. The door opened, and Natalia moved to block the doorway.

"May I come in?" Mai asked.

"If I say no, you'll, like, remind me this is your house."

"That was uncalled for."

"I don't want you to come in if you're going to tell me more lies."

"Even more uncalled for."

"Well, I don't want to be lied to."

"I'm not going to lie to you."

Natalia's eyes narrowed as she studied Mai. "If you're what I think you are, you could lie to me, and I'd never know it, right?"

"Yes, but I'm not going to lie to you."

Natalia glanced over Mai's shoulder. "You're up here by yourself, which means Popi doesn't agree with you."

"Popi doesn't know I'm up here."

The girl considered for a few moments, her face still showing skepticism, but she stepped back to let Mai enter. Natalia went to her desk, shut off the computer, then sat down and looked up at Mai.

Mai closed the door—no need to broadcast to Alexei what she was doing.

She walked to the bed and sat down, noting the chaos of books, clothes, and stuffed animals around her. She thought about chiding but decided not to.

In a gesture reminiscent of her grandfather, Natalia crossed her arms. "All right, I'm listening."

"The time you found me bleeding in the bathroom?" Natalia nodded. "Your grandfather was changing the bandage because I'd been shot."

The girl's eyes widened. Her arms fell to her sides as she leaned forward. "Someone shot you? Like, with a gun?"

"Well, it wasn't a peashooter."

"But, why?"

"He didn't want me to turn him in to the authorities, so he shot me."

"Did the police get him?"

Mai phrased the reply with care. "Yes, the police took him away." In a body bag, where I put him.

"The time that Popi was hurt in Kansas City and you came to the hospital—we were there because we were trying to stop the man who bombed the building."

Natalia's mouth gaped. "You know that guy?"

"Yes, I do."

"How did you know he was going to blow up that building?"

"I pretended to be friends with him. Because we were friends, he told me things."

"But you couldn't stop him."

A wave of bad memories and disappointment washed over her. "No, I couldn't. I tried, but sometimes a person can believe in something so much, something wrong even, that can be stronger than friendship."

Mai watched as Natalia's discomfort grew. It was one thing to want to know something and another to have the harsh truth given to you.

"I don't think I want you to tell me anymore," Natalia said.

"Too late. You're the one who started this, and I've never let you back out on something you've started."

"I'm afraid…" She stopped and gnawed her lower lip.

"You're afraid Popi and I might turn out to be different from what you've known all your life." Natalia nodded. "Well, we're not. We're the same as we've always been. We try to stop people from doing bad things. At the same time we love you, as we always have. That will never change, no matter what we do in our work."

"So, why do you do it?"

"This may sound hokey to you, but we do it to make the world a better place."

Natalia could be as manipulative as any teenager, and Mai could envision Natalia's holding this knowledge over her and Alexei's heads at the next adolescent uprising.

"All right," Mai said. "I've trusted you with this for the very reason I know I can trust you." Mai wasn't above being manipulative herself—that skill was bread and butter in her profession. "You must understand how important it is that this remains between you and me. You're smart enough to figure out why."

Natalia nodded but didn't speak.

"And Popi will be upset you and I talked about this. I'm not asking you to be dishonest with him. If you think about this for a while and decide you have other questions, I'll be happy to try and answer them. Deal?"

Natalia's reply was soft but sincere. "Deal."

"All right, then, when's this Career Day?"

"Next Wednesday at ten."

"I'll be there." Mai gave her a conspiratorial smile. "I'll even come in a limo if you think that will put the point across."

"God, no! That would be, like, totally embarrassing." She paused, thoughtful again. "But you can talk about your airplane."

"That part's easy. Would it be less embarrassing if I had the pilots do a flyover?"

The girl's eyes gleamed at that prospect, and Mai was amused at the vagaries of teenagers.

"Well, then, I hope my willingness to confide in you was helpful. However, you hurt Popi's feelings when you accused us of lying to you."

"I know. I'm sorry, and, thanks, I guess."

Mai smiled and stood, looking down into a face no longer a girl's, but a woman's. How much had the knowledge she'd received contributed to that? Mai brushed Natalia's cheek with her fingers and turned to go.

When Mai reached the doorway, Natalia called to her. "Mums?"

Surprised because Natalia hadn't called her that in a long time, Mai turned, her hand on the doorknob.

"I have one more question, and I won't ask anymore."

Mai watched as she formed the question, and she anticipated what it would be.

"Mums, have you or Popi ever killed anyone?"

Knowing silence would answer the question, Mai closed the door and shut Natalia away with the knowledge she had sought.

* * *

In their office Mai saw Alexei lounging on one of the sofas facing the French doors that led to a deck and their back yard. Beyond that was the

Potomac River, more than a mile wide at this point and swollen with early fall rains. Alexei held a snifter of brandy, a bit early in the day for it, but Mai understood. One might not taste bad right now.

Natalia had been correct, though Mai would never tell her. This day was inevitable, but that didn't make it easy to sit with someone whose values you were molding and tell her you sometimes did bad things in the name of good.

When Mai was Natalia's age, she had chosen her life's work, and the days of questioning it were long past. She had never wavered in her duty.

She crossed the room and sat by Alexei to share the view he studied with narrowed eyes. For almost a quarter hour they sat thus, their own thoughts for company. Alexei broke the silence.

"You told her."

His voice was devoid of emotion, and that was bothersome. When he retreated to that place to be the person who had been called "Ice," she actually preferred his anger. Anger meant he was capable of feeling. The other persona was known for his lack of that human attribute.

"No details. Enough for her to understand. She also understands the need to be prudent."

"I forbade it, but you did it anyway."

After all these years, why does that surprise you, she wondered.

"I did what I thought was best for her."

He didn't reply, didn't react.

"She was right. This day was coming, but we operated in a state of denial, thinking our lame excuses would count forever," Mai said.

"I never, never wanted any of this to touch her."

"An example of that denial."

The anger emerged. "Fuck you."

She would take his anger and deal with it. In a few days it would pass, and he would understand and accept what she'd done. Right now, though, he got up and walked away from her, out of the room, to another part of the house where she wasn't. That would continue for a day or so. That, and turning his back to her in bed.

She would do what she always did—be patient. Neither of them could take emptiness for long.

BLOOD VENGEANCE

1

January 16, 1999
Raçak, Kosovo

The snow-covered hills provided camouflage for the white trucks that wended their way along the hilly road. Only the letters U.N. in contrasting black on each door identified the big, Mercedes cargo trucks. They kicked up no dust on the frozen ground, though the rumble of their diesel engines told the villagers new interlopers would soon arrive.

Led by a white, U.N. Bradley Armored Vehicle, the convoy stopped in the heart of Raçak and found empty streets. The trucks' engines idling behind him, the Bradley gunner scanned with his laser-guided aiming system. On the passenger side of the lead truck, a door opened, and a pair of booted feet emerged, the wearer sliding out to land in snow. It was a woman, clad all in black, an easy target against the pale background. Her leather coat, belted at the waist, hung to mid-shin, and she was hatless in the cold, her breath frosting the air before her. Behind dark glasses, her eyes mimicked the Bradley gunner and shifted left and right, taking in the vacant streets.

The village hadn't been "cleansed" because its buildings were intact, none burned, none bombed, the mosque undefiled. A chill coursed up the woman's spine, not from the cold but from the possibilities of what—or who—had emptied the village.

U.N. Representative Maitland "Mai" Fisher walked to the left side of the Bradley where the gunner sat.

"What do you see?" she asked.

The gunner glanced again at his display. "They're there."

Eyes still on the move, Fisher walked into the sunlight, where those peering from their windows could see she was someone they knew. She stood for several, long moments, her eyes studying the distant hills, knowing she would never see the sniper, if there were one. She would feel the bullet before she heard the shot.

To her left, something creaked. Her head turned toward the sound. The dark opening of a doorway framed an older woman in a traditional head scarf. Her eyes, sunk in rolls of wrinkles, squinted in the glare from the snow. A hand came up to shade her eyes, and she made eye contact with Fisher.

"Ah!" the grandmother said. "Ah! Ah!"

She began to shout, alternating between Serbo-Croation and Albanian, as she trotted into the middle of the road where Fisher stood. When she reached Fisher, she clasped her hands in supplication and babbled, tears streaming down her face.

Other women poured from doors all about the street and converged on the two women. Their voices added to the grandmother's and went beyond Fisher's ability to translate, though her Serbo-Croatian was good. Their intent was obvious, though. They pointed to something beyond the village, and they tugged at Fisher's expensive clothes and pushed her in that direction.

The grandmother took her by the arm. "Come, come."

Fisher followed, and as she did, she looked back over her shoulder and noticed the absence of men.

Old the woman might have been, but her stride was sure-footed. She pushed forward, towing Fisher behind her, her vocalizations pleading followed by sobbing. The closer they came to a small gully with steep sides, the Grandmother's weeping increased to wails. Ten meters away, the Grandmother stopped, covered her eyes, and dropped to her knees. Her head bowed, face behind her hands, she rocked back and forth, then pointed to the gully.

Fisher felt the dread settle on her shoulders. As she walked to where the Grandmother pointed, her feet dragged. She suspected what she was about to see.

Before she saw it, she smelled it, and it brought the hackles up on her neck. Fisher slipped a hand inside her coat and brought out a gun. She gripped it in two hands to clear the way before her and continued to the gully's mouth.

The odors intensified. Not putrefaction. Too cold for that. Gunpowder. Sweat. Feces. Urine. Blood. A combination she knew and well: They were the smells of fear. Fisher saw a foot minus a shoe, the shoe nearby. Then another foot, its leg, the whole body, then another body and another. The full view of the gulley lay open to her.

Bodies, dozens of them. Sprawled. Men and boys. Dark, dried blood on the snow, on their clothing, their faces. Chests blown open. Unseeing eyes stared skyward. Slack mouths. Pale skin the color of death.

Fisher's knowing eyes studied the lay of the corpses, how they had fallen. The narrowness of the gully hemmed them in so they lay like toppled dominos, one torso resting on the legs of the body next to it. The snow was disturbed only around the bodies, and the bodies all had patches of snow on their knees. The soft sound of the Grandmother's weeping the only sound in the forest, Fisher looked up at the crest of the gully and "saw" the soldiers standing there, their automatic rifles and machine guns pointed down into the narrow wound in the earth.

The dread evaporated, and rage replaced it.

Addicted to the blood of their ethnic cleansing in Bosnia and Croatia, Slobodan Milosevic's finest, certainly no more than a day before, had slaked their cravings, four years unfulfilled, with Kosovars.

She could already hear the excuses from Belgrade. These people were rebels or aided rebels or got caught in the crossfire between the rebels and the army.

Crossfire hadn't done this, and the wounds showed they'd all been shot in the back.

The spin doctors would deliver their sound bites with straight faces and pleas for understanding the problems faced by a legitimate government dealing with a rebel liberation army and a populace who supported it in defiance of law.

Fisher put her back to the scene that would haunt her dreams for weeks and walked to the crying grandmother.

The grandmother composed herself and looked up. "My husband. My son. My grandson." She pointed to the gully again.

Fisher helped the woman to her feet and steadied her as they walked back to the village. There, the grandmother led her to the mosque. Four more bodies lay under white cloths. They hadn't been killed there but dragged here from the gully to be wept over by women. An age-old story in this part of the world where blood vengeance was the rule of law. Men kill. Women weep.

Except the dark eyes of Mai Fisher no longer wept for the dead.

The grandmother led her deeper into the mosque. On its open floor, women tended a dozen wounded. The mosque had been defiled after all. Fisher walked to and knelt by a pre-pubescent boy, shot in the leg. She examined the makeshift bandage, lifting it to peer at the wound. The boy would live, but the leg was beyond saving. As she replaced the cloth covering the ruined leg, she gave him a smile of encouragement.

Eyes red-rimmed and fatigued, the beleaguered mother looked at her.

"My son."

Her tone was defeated, already accepting a fate that wasn't certain. The boy looked from Fisher to his mother, then spoke.

"He asks if you are the Angel of Bosnia," the mother said.

"No, I'm no angel." She gave a shadow of a smile.

"You know who did this," the mother said, defeat replaced by defiance.

The women exchanged a look, the mother's eyes asking Fisher for something.

Fisher nodded and stood. The grandmother plucked at her sleeve and pointed to the bodies. "I tell everyone to leave bodies out there so world can see."

And the world did see. Later that day, summoned by Mai Fisher, the international observers and investigators arrived with the international press, whose cameras recorded the horror and the humanity of a previously unknown and unheralded Raçak, the world's newest killing ground.

2

February 27, 1999
Belgrade, Serbia

The soldier woke with a big head. Certainly not the first warrior in such a condition nor the last. As painful consciousness returned to him, he recalled how he had gotten the hangover. There had been a woman, of course. A dark-haired, dark-eyed woman. Older than he but good-looking, excited by his uniform, by the way he looked in it.

He had been granted his first liberty in months, and he and his friends had needed release from duty, honor, and country. While the diplomats talked in France, the soldiers had bar-hopped, enjoying the applause and free drinks offered to heroic defenders of the Serb Republic, and prowled for easy women.

Youngest and best-looking, Djavo Ladic had been the first to find one such woman, a European, wealthy by her clothes and jewelry. From the beginning of their encounter, she had made it obvious it was Djavo she was interested in, so his comrades had drifted away, envious and anticipating the tales he would tell.

Heady from his first battles, Djavo and the woman had drunk and talked and laughed as she let him take some liberties, then more. So much so, Djavo had worried he'd drunk too much, but, then, he'd been six months without this kind of woman, a willing one.

Like his fellow soldiers, he had taken women in many of the villages they had cleansed, but that had been as easy as taking their meager belongings. They were the spoils of war, but now he had begun to sense what he wanted from this woman could not be had by force, that it would be better not that way.

And this woman was older, more experienced, and so could help him if he lagged.

At two in the morning, they had reeled into her hotel room, and she had pulled his great coat down off his shoulders, trapping his arms. Her mouth closed on his, her tongue insistent. Djavo had wanted to free his arms so he could pull away her clothes, but her grip had been unyielding.

Now, there was only a hangover and no clear memory of their coupling. He hoped the woman was still around and wanted him as much in the daylight as she had in the dark. To wake himself, Djavo stretched.

And found he could not move.

No, he could move, but not much. As awareness now rushed in with his adrenaline, he felt the restraints on his wrists and ankles. He tested them again.

"Fight them, and they get tighter."

He recognized the woman's voice. Djavo swallowed down his panic. He was a soldier after all. Maybe the woman liked this kind of thing. What was it called? Bondage. Djavo remembered her, dressed in black, wearing a long, black leather coat. Yes, that must be it.

That thought warmed his groin, and he blinked his eyes to clear them. He looked down at his lap and realized he was bound, naked, to a chair. The headache pounded harder, but he lifted his head and willed his eyes to focus some more.

The woman sat across from him, lounging in a much more comfortable chair than the hard one he was tied to. One of her legs crossed the other at the knee, that leg swinging in small arcs. In her hands she held a cup and saucer, and she sipped from the cup in a way that was almost dainty. She was dressed the same as the night before, though she looked none the worse for all she had drunk.

His own head now clear of drink, Djavo realized she had consumed little alcohol, though she had been generous in buying him round after round. Panic rose again.

"This is what you like, yes?" he asked, a smile on his dry lips, his voice hoarse.

She didn't answer. She set the teacup aside and fixed a stare on him.

"What is this?" he demanded. Some of the bully came back to him, the bluster that brought fear to the Kosovars he encountered.

"Requital," she said.

"For what?"

"Raçak."

"Raçak? I, I wasn't there."

"Lie to me and you make it worse."

"Why do you care about Raçak?"

The woman said nothing.

"I won't talk about Raçak."

"Then, as I said, so much the worse for you."

She stood, and Djavo looked up at her, seeking the face of the woman who had laughed and touched him the night before. Her eyes had been bright and glassy, but now they were expressionless. She reached into a pocket and took out a small knife, thumbing its blade open.

She leaned over him, the knife in his face. "I see that you're not circumcised, Djavo." Her voice was low, almost a whisper, so only he could hear.

Djavo managed a nervous laugh. She had to be joking, but her eyes told him otherwise. "You're crazy."

"And what is lining up people in a gully and back-shooting them?"

"I told you, I wasn't there."

"You're lying. Last night you bragged that your unit was there."

The blade was between them as a reminder, close enough he could see how sharp it was.

"My unit was there." He compressed his lips to hold back the terror that welled again. "I did no shooting. I stayed back in the village."

"Give me the names." Djavo shook his head. "They were in your unit. You know them. I'm not practiced at this kind of surgery. One little slip, and there goes the next generation of Ladics."

"I'm a soldier. I only obey my orders. The men who did..." Djavo clenched his teeth to stop his words. He was being truthful. He had not participated in the shooting at Raçak, though some of his friends had.

As per the standing orders, all males of military age had been gathered and marched away from the village. He had heard the automatic weapons fire and seen his comrades return, laughing and joking. Later, they boasted of it.

The woman leaned closer. "Which men?" Her eyes went from his to the knife to his lap and back up to his eyes again. He pursed his lips and shook his head. "Do you know who I am?" she asked. "I have a name in Bosnia, given to me by some of your compatriots who followed orders there."

Djavo blinked at her. He had been too young for the army during Bosnia. Some of the veterans in his unit had told him of a U.N. person who called herself a relief worker but whom the Muslims called the Angel of Bosnia. The paramilitaries, however, had a different name for her because of her unrelenting pursuit of them by legal means and otherwise.

They called her the Angel of Death.

"My God," he breathed.

"That's right, Djavo. I am your god, now, with all the powers of life and death. To save your life, you give me the names."

"So you can kill them?"

His question surprised her. "Of course not. I work for the War Crimes Tribunal. Its investigators are studying the forensics from Raçak, and when they reach the inevitable conclusion, they'll need names. Do you know why men are circumcised as babies, Djavo? Because there are relatively few blood vessels in the penis then. I could be completely successful in removing the foreskin, but you could bleed to death here, tied up, naked, in a chair. What an ignoble end for a soldier. What a way to be found by the hotel maid. The soldier, the man of action, though a bit less manly than he used to be."

He looked into her eyes again. She had done this before, been close to someone she had killed. He read it there, as he had in the eyes of his fellow soldiers.

"In Raçak," he said, "the Serbian special operations entered after we took the village without a shot. A dozen of them. They picked out the rebels from the village, and they asked for my unit's veterans." His eyes on the knife, he rattled off their names. "My sergeant passed me over, but the special operations guys, we never heard their names."

"Did anyone address their leader by rank?"

He nodded. "Major."

The woman straightened and held the knife at her side. Her stare made him blink, and she walked out of Djavo's sight.

"What, what are you going to do with me?"

"Let you go," came her voice.

"You're lying."

"No, not now. I lied when I said I wanted you, but you didn't seem to notice. By the way, if you're thinking of reporting this..."

The room's television/VCR came on, and Djavo saw himself, trussed to the chair and spilling his guts. She said nothing, but Djavo understood. Everyone in his unit would get a copy, maybe even someone in the special operations command, if he said a word of this.

She walked to the VCR and removed the cassette and went out of his sight again. Dvajo couldn't stop a shiver when he felt her hand on his neck, her breath there as she leaned down. One of his hands came free. She had cut his bonds, but the knife point was at his throat.

"I'll be leaving now," she said. "You can finish untying yourself. Your clothes are here. Get dressed and forget this, but you have my permission to tell your friends I was the best you ever had."

The point of the knife left his throat. When he got up the courage to look around, she was gone.

March 22, 1999
Kosovar Refugee Camp, Albania

The tradition was for another male family member to take in her and her son now that her husband was dead. With only one leg, her son moved too slowly on his crutches, and the mother feared she would never reach her husband's uncle. She was a strong woman, but the boy was twelve. No longer could she carry him, and when she tried, it only humiliated him.

U.N. doctors had amputated his leg above the knee, and the woman— the relief worker—who had brought the news of Raçak to the world had made sure the boy got medicines and the crutches. On the relief worker's last visit to Raçak, she had promised a prosthesis, but soon after the woman and her son fled with many others to seek security with relatives in Albania.

It was now Spring, though a fresh snowfall added to the refugees' woes. No help came from Albania, whose government had to keep them at arm's length and insist they were illegals or risk the might of the Serb Army, now running unchecked in Kosovo, being turned on them. There was only the food people had carried with them, and most of that had been confiscated at the border.

At first, when the mother heard trucks approach, she thought they were Serbian tanks, defying the border to kill them all. Her son was the one to reassure her. He hopped on one leg and held his crutch in the air.

"It's her! It's her!" he shouted to his mother.

Almost too weary to do so, the mother stood up from her makeshift tent and shielded her eyes against the snow-glare. U.N. trucks. At least there would be food and blankets.

"It's only relief workers," she told her son.

The boy was insistent. "She said she would come. Can I go see?"

"No."

"But how will she know where we are?"

"It was a promise made from guilt, like all the westerners. They promise but do nothing. Don't get your hopes up."

Even as she spoke, the mother studied the people emerging from the trucks. The refugees surged toward them, and the mother put a hand on her son's shoulder to keep him back.

Then, she was there. The woman. Dressed in black again. The same long, leather coat. She stood amid the ragged humanity who reached out to her. The mother watched as she made her way across the camp.

"I'm no angel," the woman had once said, but she was the very image of it now to the mother.

A man limped beside the woman, and he carried a box perhaps a meter long. He and the woman searched the faces around them as they strode through the camp. The mother felt her son slip from her grasp and watched him move forward on his crutches to meet the woman. She must have heard his shouts because she looked toward him and smiled. The mother watched her son reach the woman's side, and the woman stroked his hair. She left her hand on his shoulder until the three of them arrived by the quilt the mother had suspended between two trees for their shelter.

"Mother," the woman greeted. "I came back to Raçak and was told you'd left. I didn't think I would find you."

"It was too dangerous there," the mother replied.

The woman motioned to her companion. "This is a friend of mine from America. We have something for the boy."

The man smiled and opened the box. Inside was a prosthetic leg, a small one; a child's leg. The mother thought it both the ugliest thing she'd ever seen and the most beautiful.

"I lost my leg in Africa," the man explained. "I stepped on a land mine. I can show the boy how to use it, care for it."

"I have no money," the mother said. Her son's face grew sad.

"It's a gift," the other woman said. "If you tell me where you're going to live, I'll make sure he gets others as he grows." The woman leaned down to the boy, who was wide-eyed with joy and struggled not to weep. "If you go with my friend, he'll teach you all about your new leg."

The boy looked to his mother. She hesitated. Trust was the first thing she had lost after the Serbs came to her village on a cold, January morning, but today hope constricted her throat. She could only nod.

The man closed the box and motioned the boy to follow him. Alone, the two women regarded each other much as they had in the mosque two months before.

"I have something for you, too," the woman told the mother.

"For me, I want nothing."

"You'll want this."

The woman reached inside her leather coat, withdrew a package wrapped in brown paper, and held it out toward the mother. The mother took it with some trepidation and began to unwrap it.

On the day when hell came to Raçak, the Serbian special forces had arrived, clad in their winter camouflage—white pants and white pullover, hooded jackets—worn over their uniforms. The wrapping fell away, and the mother held up one of those white jackets, except the front of this one was crusted in dried blood as if the wearer's throat...

The women looked at each other again, and the mother knew this was what she had asked for without words, what no woman in her culture could request, the traditional blood vengeance. The mother had asked it of a stranger, this woman, because she had no husband to avenge her son.

"And what will you do?" the mother asked, not knowing she echoed a hapless Serb soldier. "Kill them all?"

"No. One was enough."

"Why for my son?"

"It wasn't only for your son."

"Why?"

"I'll never know why. I came to the Balkans to try and bring peace. I hate it here, and I love it here. It made me what I am."

The mother looked at her trophy, folded it carefully, and re-wrapped it in the paper. She tucked it away in the suitcase she had carried from Raçak.

She turned around to thank the woman but saw her walking away, again engulfed by other refugees, their outstretched hands trying to touch her but sliding off the black leather coat without gaining purchase.

A FATHER'S NO SHIELD FOR HIS CHILD

1

Washington, D.C.

To keep warm in the chill, November air, William Henry Munro paced. A drizzle fell, and though his overcoat was warm and waterproof, his head was bare. The tips of his ears were uncomfortably cold and, he suspected, as red as his chapped cheeks.

At forty-two he was of an age where a man started to get vain about his looks, worried about his hair, concerned about his weight, but Munro had a thick head of hair, salt and pepper in color, cut conservatively. His work demanded he stay lean and fit.

A few women he'd dated had called him attractive, never handsome, and he couldn't judge for himself. His northern European skin, sensitive to extremes of cold and heat, had always vexed him. He was sure he looked like he'd been on a twenty-four-hour drunk. On a day like today, in addition to the ruddiness, his nose would run like a faucet.

On cue, it did. He reached for his handkerchief, to keep his upper lip from embarrassment, and glanced around, his eyes seeking.

The dismal day hadn't deterred tourists from the Vietnam Veterans Memorial. Only a few days away from Veterans Day, there were already lots of commemorative events. People arrived early, had impromptu reunions, and placed their remembrances at the wall of black granite etched with names from another generation.

Munro had missed out on Vietnam, his birth date making him eligible for the lottery, not the draft, and he'd drawn a high number. He'd been in college in 1975 when the U.S. retreated from Saigon, and he was among that group of baby boomers who had never entered military service because

33

it wasn't mandatory. He had weathered the derision of the vets at his workplace, who deemed him incapable of being a Secret Service Agent because he hadn't fought Charlie.

He'd been an agent for more than twenty years, he got all the promotions exactly when they should have come, the old guys had retired, and the Secret Service itself was now more reflective of America. That was a good thing, even if a few holdovers from the "good old days" thought otherwise.

The breeze picked up and chilled him even more. He waited for a woman, one who'd said she'd meet him between 1300 and 1330 right here at the Vietnam Women's Memorial on the high ground above the black slash in the earth that was The Wall. He checked his watch. 1326.

Munro began his scan again, his impatience rising. His training made him push it down, but that was becoming harder as the minutes ticked past. He glanced down at the crepe paper poppy she'd told him to purchase from a vendor so she'd recognize him. Or any of the couple hundred other people wearing one.

Because of his training, a movement caught his attention, and he focused on a woman striding toward him from the direction of the Washington Monument. He took a moment to admire the swing of her hips and studied the rest of her. Clad all in black, down to a supple, leather trench coat worn unbelted, she had donned sunglasses on the overcast day. She wore her hair loose, unlike when he'd seen her before, and as she neared Munro saw she was little changed in four years. Her dark hair had two gray streaks, one at each temple, but Munro thought it a striking feature, so striking he wondered if she wore them uncolored on purpose. Yet, Munro remembered her as unassuming about her appearance, and he decided having the gray streaks so prominent meant she didn't care how they looked.

He saw the firm set of her mouth and was disconcerted because he couldn't read her eyes behind the sunglasses. As a Secret Service agent he hated not being able to see a subject's eyes.

She turned a few heads other than his on her trek, and he had been so absorbed in watching, he didn't realize she had stopped a few feet away.

Munro recovered and extended his right hand. "Ms. Fisher, good to see you again." She shook his hand but said nothing. "I was the Secret Service Agent…"

"Yes," she said. "In Kansas City. You were a little fresh."

He smiled and flushed. "Yes, I was. I didn't know you were married."

"Why am I here, Agent Munro?"

Munro took a moment to relish the high-class British accent. "Please, call me Hank. Ms. Fisher, may we go somewhere to talk?"

"We are somewhere, Agent Munro, and until I know why the Secret Service wants to talk to me, I prefer us right here."

Munro fidgeted, his composure threatening to leave him. He needed to approach her the right way and not resort to begging before the small talk was over. He saw her brow crease above the sunglasses.

"It's probably best to talk somewhere a little more private," he said.

"If this is about President Randolph's secretary scandal," she said, "not only do I know absolutely nothing, I can't be compelled to testify about it."

Munro flushed again. "No, it's nothing to do with that. The Secret Service doesn't what to talk to you. I do."

"This isn't official?"

"No."

"My Director indicated I was needed for a national security matter."

"I'm, uh, afraid I may have used some agency resources for a personal matter."

"The President's personal matters are no concern of mine."

"It's not the President's personal matters."

"Mr. Munro, you need to start explaining why I got called away from the Balkans, through official channels, by the way, for someone's personal matter."

"Look, I wouldn't have gone through official channels, but when I asked around in the intelligence community on how to contact you, they were pretty mum."

"That's why we're spies. You've got two more minutes of my time, Mr. Munro."

"I feel exposed here. I would rather speak somewhere more private."

"Two minutes."

"Ms. Fisher, please, I used channels because it was the only way I could be assured I could speak to you."

"About what?"

"A personal matter, one I'd rather discuss in private."

"When you talk in circles, you forfeit your time. Good day."

She turned, but before she took two steps, Munro found his voice. "Eamon Killkenny."

She whirled back, closing until she was in his face. The cold finally got to him, and he shivered. When she took off her sunglasses, he saw a mixture of emotions in her eyes, mostly suspicion. She spoke in what sounded like Russian and looked around her. She turned back to him.

"See the man in the gray coat?" she asked, nodding toward her left.

Munro looked around and saw a man standing maybe fifty feet away. He spoke into a wrist mike. When he saw Munro looking at him, he nodded. "Friend of yours?" he asked Mai.

"My husband's nephew, late of the *Spetsnaz*, currently assigned as my bodyguard. If he receives the agreed-upon signal from me, you're a dead man."

"Christ! What do you think I want with you?"

"Well, I don't know that, do I, since you haven't told me what you want."

"Why do you have a bodyguard?"

"There a quite a few Serbian generals and politicians under indictment for war crimes because of me. Recently, in Zagreb there was an attempt."

"Attempt? As in, to kill you?" She raised an eyebrow in answer. "You okay?"

"Quite well, thank you."

"Hence, the bodyguard."

"My husband now works at The Hague, and he worries needlessly about me."

"What did you call him? Spats..."

"*Spetsnaz*. Formerly the Soviet Special Forces. There were two kinds. Shock troops and assassins."

"Which one is he?"

"Shock troop, but he's very talented."

"Oh. Well, I'm not on some Serbian general's payroll." He forced a smile, but she didn't respond.

"Let's stroll, Mr. Munro, so we don't attract undue attention."

He fell in beside her, and they began to walk.

"You mentioned Eamon Cill Chainnigh," she said, giving the name its Gaelic pronunciation. "That's a name I haven't heard in a very long time. I'm curious why you mentioned an IRA hit man to me."

"I'm Irish."

"So claims ninety percent of Americans with a vaguely Irish surname."

"No, I am Irish. Was Irish. I was born there. My parents came to America when I was two and became citizens."

"So, you're Eamon's long-lost cousin, and he's hit you up for money or guns?"

"No."

"Well, Mr. Munro, I'm Irish, too. Now that we have that in common, I'd like to know how you know Cill Chainnigh."

"You're saying his name differently."

"You Americanized it—Kill-kinny. I pronounced it in Gaelic—accent on a different syllable. Tell me why you mentioned his name to me."

"He kidnapped a U.S. citizen in Ireland, and he contacted me."

"You want your brothers in the FBI."

"I'm aware of that."

"Have you contacted them?"

"No."

"Why the hell not?"

"Kilkenny said he would kill the person if I did."

Fisher shook her head in disbelief. "You've been a federal law enforcement officer for what, fifteen, twenty years?"

"Twenty-two."

"And you fell for that?"

"You don't understand."

"No, I don't, and I'm losing patience waiting for you to explain it."

"Kilkenny suggested I contact you."

"My last dealings with Cill Chainnigh were more than thirteen years ago, and I haven't worked Ireland since. Not even the Omagh bombing. Besides, Cill Chainnigh didn't know me as Mai Fisher. The person he thought I was is 'dead.'"

"He said, 'Tell her I found out she survived Lifford.'"

Mai stopped walking, her eyes staring ahead at nothing. "Fuck," she murmured.

She turned around, held a hand up to Kolya, and her eyes came back to Munro.

"All right, I know the kidnapped person isn't anyone in my family. If it were the President's daughter that would be all over the news. Since it's not anyone important to me, I'm still not sure why I'm here."

"No, the person doesn't matter to you. She matters to me."

Mai gave a throaty laugh and motioned for them to walk again. "What was it? An exchange program with the Garda and you met a little piece over in Ireland you had to have? Now, someone's claiming she's kidnapped to get something from you."

"If you'd let me finish..."

"Open your eyes, Munro. You've been had. They knew you were from the Secret Service, so they knew you'd have the means to contact someone in the intelligence community. I'm not playing the IRA's game, and neither should you. Give the President my regards. I'll forgo mentioning this to my Director."

She turned to go, but Munro put a hand on her arm. They stood, facing each other again.

"Please, let me finish," he said. "The woman is not a 'piece' I had. I'm trying to explain. It's difficult to find the words. This is beyond my control, something I couldn't go to my superiors about. I know I should have. That's how I was trained, but I couldn't react as a Secret Service agent because I had to act as a..."

Emotion stopped him again.

She peered into his face, her expression softening. "Munro, get on with it."

Munro swallowed and found his voice. "As a father." He slumped, from exhaustion, emotion, he didn't know, but Mai supported him and clasped one of his hands.

"I have to move my car," she said, "and you need a drink. Meet me at the Hay-Adams lounge in fifteen minutes."

"How do I know you'll show up?"

"Because I've said so." She turned and strode away.

Munro watched the man in the gray coat stare at him for a moment longer, and he turned and jogged to catch up with Mai Fisher.

* * *

"What do you think?" Mai asked Kolya Antonov when he reached her side.

"Trap."

"Why would the Secret Service set a trap for me?"

"Maybe not Secret Service trap. Maybe his trap."

"And I thought your uncle was the pessimistic one."

"Speaking of *Dyadya*, why isn't he here?"

"Because you're my bodyguard, and he and I still don't see eye to eye on a few issues."

"That is why I married doctor. She stays out of my business. I stay out of hers."

"That's your life, Kolya, not mine."

"Was only example, not advice. Are you going to meet this Munro?"

"I think so."

"And if it is trap?"

"That's what I pay you generously for."

"I would not meet him."

"There's a strong argument for that, but he piqued my curiosity."

"Old Russian saying—curiosity killed cat."

They reached her car and got in, Mai behind the wheel.

"You know the ending to that. Stay close in the bar and look intimidating." She started the car, put it in gear, and moved into D.C. traffic.

Kolya smiled. "You pay me generously for that, too."

* * *

A substantial tip encouraged the host to give them as much privacy as possible. A couple of barflies guzzled expensive Scotch at the bar, and the host gave Mai and Munro a table in a secluded corner of the lounge. Kolya, who had followed them, sat at the bar, but where he could see them, and ordered black coffee. Mai smiled when he flicked his throat with an index finger, indicating he'd prefer vodka.

Their coats draped over empty chairs at the table, Mai and Munro sat unspeaking until the host brought the two Irish Coffees Mai had ordered.

Munro sampled his and smiled. "Imagine my surprise when I tried to order one of these in Dublin. The publican stared at me as if I was nuts."

Mai gave the smile back.

"The Irish don't like diluting whiskey. Irish Coffee started in San Francisco, about as far from Ireland as you can get, but I have a weakness for them."

"Me too."

He drank some more, and she waited. She had pushed him hard earlier, and now that she knew why he'd been so obtuse, she regretted that. She'd have to rein in her impatience and let him set the pace.

"I was rude earlier, and I apologize, but what you've told me means you need to tell me the whole story and quickly," she said.

"I was married when I was in college."

"You want to go back that far?"

"I've got to tell it my way."

She sighed and quelled her impatience. "All right, then. You got married in college."

"Yeah, back in the days when you still made an honest woman out of your girlfriend when birth control failed."

"Happens in the best of families."

Munro's eyes, curious, came up to hers.

"Why do you think I'm married?" she said.

Munro tried to grin. "What, did you have to make an honest man out of your husband?"

Mai gave him a sincere smile. "Something like that."

"Well, with me, the pregnancy lasted longer than the marriage. My ex and I had joint custody for a couple of years, then she decided having a kid cramped her style as a Grateful Dead groupie. So, I raised our daughter."

"A single father in the Secret Service? A wonder they didn't drum you out or something."

"I had an understanding boss, thankfully. It was still hard, and there were times I should have put her first, but we worked it out. We're father and daughter, but we're buddies, too. You must know."

She didn't know. None of her pregnancies had gone to term, and she pushed away the memory. That was something Munro didn't need to know.

"I had a lot of help from my mother," he was saying. "When Deidre was little, that is. When I decided to finish out my career here in D.C., she opted to study at Catholic University. She had her own apartment in D.C., but we were still close, you know. I see her—saw her—every day."

Mai watched as Munro gripped the mug of Irish Coffee with two hands and wondered if he were still cold from the weather or from the touch of IRA madness. "Go on."

"This past Spring, her literature class or some such, read the book *Angela's Ashes*. You know it?" Mai nodded. "She knew she was half Irish. It was never a big deal until she read that book. Then, she had to go, so she and I went at spring break. She went back by herself over the summer, then applied for and got into an exchange program with Trinity College for this semester." Munro gave a genuine smile. "We were running up the trans-Atlantic phone bills, let me tell you."

He sobered again, took a long drink of his Irish Coffee, finishing it, and sat quietly again, the smile gone, a haunting on his face.

Mai wanted to tell him to get on with it but remembered to let him set the pace. She caught the host's eye and held up two fingers for another round. She heard Munro's sigh and turned back to him.

"Five days ago, I get this call from her," Munro continued. "I have to come over and right away, but she won't tell me what's wrong. She was trying to be nonchalant, but this is my kid, you know. I can read her like a book, part of my job. Then, this man comes on the phone, gives me a time and a place in Dublin and tells me I got thirty-six hours to get there. If I call the FBI, the Garda, anyone, he says, she's dead." All the emotion came into his face then. "And I hear her scream."

Mai saw the waiter approaching and put her hand on Munro's wrist. She also saw Kolya rise from the bar. She gave him a head shake, and he sat back down. When the waiter left, Mai released her hold on Munro and urged his drink toward him. He was Irish after all. Whiskey would only lubricate his mouth.

"Don't misunderstand this question, Munro. It has to be asked," she said. "How do you know she's still alive?"

"They call me every day, and I get to talk to her. And I can tell it's her, not a recording."

"Are you certain?"

"Yes!" That was defensive.

"When is the next call due?"

"Tonight. Nine o'clock."

"All right. You went to the meet in Dublin?" He nodded. "Tell me what happened."

"Kilkenny let me see her. She was hand-cuffed in the backseat of a car, with C4 and a fuse strapped to her, and Kilkenny, the IRA man, had the dead man's switch."

"Semtex."

"What?"

"Not C4. The U.S. has too tight a control on that. The IRA use Semtex now, and to be clear, Cill Chainnigh is not IRA anymore. He's a breakaway, fighting his own war now."

"I thought you said you didn't work Ireland anymore."

"I don't, but I keep abreast and do an occasional consult. Describe the man who said he was Cill Chainnigh."

"About five-seven, five-eight. Mid-sixties. Bald on top. White hair with some red in it. Grey eyes. Fleshy. On his cheeks, what do they call them, the red veins?"

"Spider veins, the bane of heavy-drinking Irishmen everywhere."

Munro's description fit a Cill Chainnigh who had aged more than a decade. When she knew him he was already going to seed. "At the meet, is that where he mentioned me?"

"Yeah. At first I thought he wanted money or for me to facilitate a shipment of guns or something along those lines."

"Did he know that you know me?"

"No. Well, he never said anything, at least, and I didn't offer it. He gave me your name, told me to find you."

"What else did he say?"

"He said to do whatever I needed to do to get you to Ireland by November 11. If I didn't, my daughter would die."

"November 11? Are you sure?"

"Yes, he was insistent. What's the significance of November 11?"

Mai didn't want to share, but Munro was a father with a child's life in the balance. "November 11 is the anniversary of an explosion that destroyed a farmhouse in Lifford, County Donegal, just over the border from Northern Ireland. Nine IRA people died in the explosion. There was one survivor."

"Did you have something to do with it?"

Letting her memory walk through a door she wanted to keep closed, she said, "In a manner of speaking."

"I would like a better answer."

"Leave it at that, Munro."

"I can't. A man kidnaps my daughter and asks me to find you. I need to know why."

"It's classified, so don't even ask again. Look, Munro, again, don't misunderstand me, but are you sure she was kidnapped?"

Munro's stare grew hostile. "What the fuck does that mean?"

"It's not the first time some dewy-eyed young girl goes to the Old Sod to find her roots but finds the IRA instead. Usually, a good-looking man talks her up in a pub. Eventually, the chat turns to The Cause, and she gets suckered in."

"No. No fucking way."

"She probably talked about you, told them proudly you're a Secret Service agent. That's access they could use. That information gets passed to Cill Chainnigh, and your daughter gets convinced to go along with a kidnapping charade."

"That was not a charade. I know my daughter."

"You were distraught, not thinking clearly."

"I. Know. My. Daughter. She was fucking scared to death. She was not acting. You said you're a mother. You know what I'm talking about."

Mai looked away from him. Had he lived, her oldest child would be twenty-one years old, and she still occasionally indulged the fantasy of whether he would look like her or Alexei. She looked back at Munro. "All right, Munro, it's a kidnapping. I had to ask, I had to make certain you were sure."

"I'm sorry."

"No problem. Now, what precisely did Cill Chainnigh tell you to do?"

"If I get you to Sligo by November 11, to a place he'll tell me once I confirm contact with you, he'll tell you, and only you, where my daughter is."

"In exchange for what?"

"You. You don't seem surprised."

"Cill Chainnigh was never very original."

"Then, you need to work out a way to find her."

"You think I can pull that information out of a back pocket?"

"You have resources…"

"Which I could tap if this were official. I told you, I haven't worked Ireland in a long time. Any sources I had are long gone, or they think I'm dead. Tell me you put a trace on the calls."

"Too much red tape."

"Christ, man, you must know how to manipulate the system."

"Of course, but Kilkenny has been careful to keep the contact well under the time it takes to trace a trans-Atlantic call."

"Well, he's a smart man." At Munro's frown she added, "Oh, he's a bastard, but a smart one. After Lifford, he left Ireland for years, lived in Libya, East Germany, North Korea, China. Frankly, I'm surprised he'd risk setting foot in Ireland again. MI-6 thought he was dead."

"You know a lot for not having worked Ireland for years."

"I do get briefings, Munro. Why has he risked setting foot in Ireland now? Why this anniversary? Why not the twentieth or the tenth?"

"What are you driving at?"

"Maybe he won't be around for the next anniversary."

"All right, I think you need to tell me more about this event in Lifford."

"I can't."

"You won't. I can tell the difference. I need to know. Dammit, this is my daughter's life." He waited for a reply he should have known wouldn't come. "He said if I delivered your body to him, he'd tell me where Deidre is."

Mai gave him a smile that made him uncomfortable.

"Kolya would never let that happen, even if I would, and how do you propose to get my body across an ocean and into another country?"

"I don't know, but I'd fucking find a way by November 11."

"Remember, Munro, at the right look from me, Kolya manages to make it look like you had a heart attack."

"And my daughter dies, and it's your fucking fault."

Ah, fuck, he had to say that. "So what?"

"You won't let it happen. You try to save lives. You tried to stop the Kansas City bombing. You won't let an innocent girl die for whatever it was you did in Lifford."

"You have no idea what I did in Lifford."

"Then, you better tell me so I'll understand why my daughter had to die because you're afraid of Eamon Kilkenny."

"Is that what you think it is?"

"What else could it be?"

"That won't work on me, Munro. You think Cill Chainnigh is going to clap me on the back and say, 'No hard feelings, old girl?'"

"Tell me why Kilkenny took my daughter. Why does he want you so bad?"

Something in Munro's posture alerted Kolya. Mai saw him coming toward the table. Instead of waving him off, Mai let him come.

Kolya hooked a chair from another table with his foot, spun it, and sat on it, his arms atop the back. He fixed his gaze on Munro but spoke in Russian to Mai.

"*Tetya*, I don't like how this looks."

Mai replied in Russian as well. "I have it under control, Kolya, but stare at him in that way you have."

Munro leaned toward her. "You think that scares me? Threatening stares, talking in Russian. From what some folks in the FBI say about you, you don't use decorative muscle to do your dirty work."

"'Decorative?'" Kolya said in English. "My muscles are real. My uncle does not like when people threaten his wife. Since I obey my uncle in all things, I think you need to be more... Ah, what is word, *tetya*? *Vezhlivyy*?"

"Polite."

"*Da*, yes. Polite. I think you need to be polite. I will go back to bar now." He did just that.

Munro didn't relent. "You know, right now, I don't care if your Russian thug kills me because if someone kills my kid, I don't want to live."

"That means you have nothing to lose."

"Yeah, it does."

Mai studied his face, his eyes rheumy from the two drinks. "A man with nothing to lose is dangerous."

"Fucking A." He blinked and sat back in his chair. "Sorry. They make their drinks a little strong here."

"Fucking A," Mai murmured. "Have you ever done any undercover work?"

"No."

"All right, I'm only going to say this once—what I'm about to tell you is classified, and I'm twisting the rules about that because this shanty Irish bastard Cill Chainnigh has you by the balls. I was undercover in the IRA for six months. My organization, my husband, the British government considered it a suicide mission, but I was determined to prove them wrong. My job was to get in and secure enough faith to be trusted with a shipment of Semtex, nearly a hundred pounds of it."

"Explosives and the IRA. Big surprise."

"Do you have any idea what a hundred pounds of Semtex can do?"

"Create a pretty big hole, I would think."

"Not one blast, Munro. A lot of small ones. In train stations. Shopping malls. Ascot. Wimbledon. MI-6 knew it had been purchased for the IRA, and they knew which IRA cell would receive it."

"The one you were in?"

"Yes."

"Why didn't they intercept the shipment?"

"Not enough. They wanted to know how many other cells it would be divided among and where they were going to use it."

"So that was your job?"

She nodded. "And once I passed that on, I was to destroy the shipment before it got broken up and dispersed."

"How did you get in?"

"I spent months learning the history of a woman jailed here in the States for running guns to the IRA. Her father and Cill Chainnigh were lads together before the father took his daughter to the U.S. and taught her how to run guns. The father died in prison, and prison tempered the woman's enthusiasm for The Cause. MI-6 learned she was going into witness protection and wanted her help before they could no longer get access to her."

"She agreed?"

"She was done with the IRA. She and I had a superficial resemblance, enough to fool Cill Chainnigh, who hadn't seen her since she was five or six. When the time came to deport her, the U.S. Marshals and MI-6 swapped me in for her, and Eamon Cill Chainnigh welcomed me with open arms, like a long-lost daughter of his own."

"That easy?"

"Most Irishmen are a sentimental lot, terrorist or no. He sent me to his cell since they were down one. We lived in a farmhouse in the countryside near Lifford. They let me in on Eamon's word, and no one was the wiser. He trusted me like he'd trusted his friend, dead in America, and gave me the Semtex. Then, he gave me the distribution list—ten pounds each to ten cells, ours included."

"The Semtex was in the farmhouse?" She nodded. "No wonder it blew up."

"Semtex is not as stable as C4, and under the right conditions, it'll sweat nitroglycerin, but it needs a detonator. The detonators were with the shipment."

Mai paused and drank some of her coffee. It was near the bottom of the mug, where the sugar and whiskey were the strongest. Amnesia had put most of this out of her mind, and other horrors had superseded it. The telling of it brought it back again. She drained the mug and resumed her story.

"I was able to get a copy of the distribution list to my contact at my next check-in time, but MI-6 didn't want me to blow the shipment before I could learn when the Semtex would be distributed."

"Wait, who cares when? They knew you had the whole shipment, and they knew who was going to receive it. When didn't matter."

"So I thought, but they didn't. There was no way to know if I'd get that information in time to get it to them before the distribution, and in fact that's what happened. Cill Chainnigh sent a courier with the message to start the distribution—on a date before from my next check-in. So, I did what had to be done—risk ten lives to save hundreds. But when you live with people for months, people who on the surface look like the people you grew up with, it's hard to risk even those lives. I decided I was the only person who needed to die."

She picked up her mug, remembered it was empty, and put it down, her hands still clutching it.

"I thought I set the timer for when everyone would be out of the house. It was a working farm, after all. But the bloody bomb blew early."

"Jesus…"

She held up a hand to stop him. "Because of that 'little' failure, the IRA military council thought it best that Cill Chainnigh leave the country for a while."

Mai toyed with the empty mug, feeling a yen for something she'd given up a while ago—cocaine. She pushed it away as she shoved the mug aside.

"So, Agent Munro, that's why he took your daughter. He's using you and yours to get to me so I can atone for the nine people I murdered."

"But it was an accident, right?"

She smiled with some irony. "Someone else said the same thing."

"Your husband?"

"No. The Kansas City bomber."

45

"You told him, and I had to beg?"

"In his case, it was an object lesson. For you, it's another classified story. Who'd believe him, anyway?" She pointed to her mug. "Do you want another?"

"No."

"Well, then, I'll look like a drunk if I do." She took a money clip from a pocket and pulled a twenty and a ten away, dropping them on the table. "Make my day and tell me you've taped your conversations with Cill Chainnigh."

Munro gave her a half-hearted smile. "My head's halfway screwed on."

She handed him a business card. "Good. That's my home address. After your call tonight, come there and bring your tapes. In the meantime, I'll see what I can find out, quasi-officially."

"Then what?"

"Then, you and I take my plane to Ireland and fulfill your obligation to Cill Chainnigh, with a few modifications on his plan, of course."

"Thank you," Munro said, and Mai feared he was about to weep. If he did, they'd both be blubbering, and Kolya would laugh.

"Best not to thank me yet."

"Why?"

"Because you're going to owe me big time."

2

The Hague, Netherlands

Alexei Bukharin watched the woman on the witness stand break down, sobbing, gasping, trembling. He supposed even with your rapist under guard, sitting in the same room with him was daunting. The judge ordered a brief recess while a nurse attended to the distraught woman. A noise caught Alexei's attention. The defendant, a Serb in his thirties, was sniggering, ignoring his lawyer's admonition to keep quiet. Alexei fixed his eyes on the back of the man's head and wished he could bore holes.

"Your Honor?" said the nurse. "The witness has seriously elevated blood pressure. She needs to be sedated."

Judge Amelie Richardson checked with the two junior judges on the panel and slammed her gavel down. "Court is recessed until 0900 tomorrow morning."

Richardson stood up, caught Alexei's eye, and nodded toward the door leading to her chambers.

Alexei rose, and when he neared the defendant's seat, he heard him say, "They can't possibly think I'd put it in that dog."

Alexei hooked his foot around a leg of the defendant's chair and pulled it out from under him. The startled man landed hard on his ass, and Alexei smiled. "Sorry, I didn't see you there."

The defendant started to get up, but the guards moved in and subdued him.

"Was that really an appropriate action for the Secretary General's Special Liaison?" asked the defense lawyer.

"I'm sorry I didn't break his neck."

"Mr. Bukharin, my client is innocent until proven guilty."

"Yes, that's the law, and it's a good law. But I'm the one who liberated his rape camp. I know what I know."

Alexei strode away toward the door the judge indicated. He tapped lightly and entered.

Amelie had shed her robes and sat behind her desk, long fingers massaging her temples. She looked up at Alexei. "Is it too early for a drink?"

Alexei smiled and shook his head. "For the Scotch you keep here? Never too early. Keep your seat. I'll pour."

Aware Amelie's eyes were on him, Alexei went to the dry bar and poured two glasses of Scotch, neat.

"Thanks, Alexei. You look like hell, by the way. Don't you sleep?"

"Do you?"

"It's tough, let me tell you, after hearing things like we heard today. Tougher for me because I'm a woman, I suppose."

Alexei handed her a glass and sat in a chair before the desk. "I think it's difficult for anyone, man or woman, to hear that the pain and humiliation linger even years later."

"How do people who were neighbors, hell, in-laws, for generations turn on each other?"

"I think you're in a unique position to understand that."

"Alexei, blacks and whites in the South when I was a kid might have lived near each other, but the white folks never considered us neighbors."

"Same hatred. Different ethnic group."

"How do you do it? Look at the evil you've seen and not be affected by it?"

"Don't assume I'm not affected. It's called compartmentalization."

"Well, my grandmere, she were a swamp witch, and she always said never let a wound fester."

"My mother wasn't a witch, just full of good sense, and she said much the same thing. I usually have Mai nearby to vent with."

"So, I know why I don't sleep, though my good-looking husband does his best to relax me. Why aren't you sleeping?"

"Who knows? Old age?"

"Loneliness?"

Alexei shrugged and drank Scotch.

"Do you know where she is?" Amelia asked.

"In a tent or a barracks in Serbia or Croatia or Bosnia. Who knows? Back at our house in America. I'm not her favorite person right now."

"Why? 'Cause you wanted to stop doing all that dangerous shit?"

He shrugged again and nodded.

"Have you talked to her?"

"Her cell phone has Caller ID, so I get her voice mail."

"Damn."

Alexei rolled the glass between his hands and stared at its contents. "You know, the other day, I looked around the house I rented here, the one I rented for us, and I realized there's nothing of hers there. No cast-off underwear, no lipstick or earring left behind, nothing to show I have a wife. It's as if she doesn't exist." He drained his Scotch, upset he had bared too much.

"Take some time off. Mend fences," Amelie told him.

"I'm always the one who crawls back. Not this time."

"Cherie, if you're gonna wait on a woman to set aside her pride and crawl back, you could wait a long time."

"Oh, I'm well aware, so I'm certain I'll go ahead and relent. I need to indulge my own pride a while longer."

"Well, you can get some sleep and stop living off coffee."

Alexei lifted the empty glass. "Maybe I'll switch to this. Much better than coffee, which the doctor did say I was drinking too much of."

"What were you at the doctor for?"

"Why did you call me in here?"

"Because you look like you're about to drop. Why were you at the doctor?"

"To get something to help me sleep. My blood pressure was elevated. Not much, but out of my normal range. He asked if anything unusual was going on in my life."

He and Amelie shared a laugh. "And you said?"

"Oh, nothing unusual at all, doctor. I sit day after day and listen to horrific accounts of torture, rape, murder—some of which I witnessed and couldn't stop—and my wife of twenty-one years prefers to spook about Eastern Europe rather than live with me."

"Sounds like the life of a retired spy."

"He said much the same."

"Why did you retire?"

"I've survived a long time in this business, and there were times when I almost didn't. I saw the signs. Slower reflexes. Reading glasses. I didn't want to be a liability to my partner."

"That would be your partner and wife, the adrenaline junkie?"

"Oh yes, and there was a time when I'd use that in her to my advantage. When I wanted to take fewer chances, she wanted to take more. Our lives have become full circle. We switched roles."

"Ain't love grand?"

"Oh, yes, the grandest."

"Do you doubt she loves you?"

"Sometimes. Right now, in particular."

Amelie leaned back in her chair, studying him, and Alexei didn't like the scrutiny.

"You know," Amelia began, "what I know of Mai, I know she'd be even more pissed at this self-emasculation. Go for a walk, Alexei. Go to the gym and take your frustration out on a punching bag. Do something other than sit here and drink my good Scotch, that is, when you're not crying in it. So you're a retired spy approaching sixty with a marriage on the rocks. Welcome to the real world. Now, get up. Do something about it."

Alexei set his empty glass on the desk and rose, smiling. "You know, you sound a lot like my mother."

"Why, thank you, and you at least listen, unlike my own, ungrateful offspring."

Alexei headed for the door.

"Alexei?"

"Look, Amelie, the lecture was enough, really."

"One more piece of advice. Fix that marriage up and soon, 'cause there's a torpedo headed your way named Anne Hobard."

"The chief prosecutor?"

"And a better one I haven't found, but you haven't noticed the sly glances and flirty remarks?"

Alexei decided he must be getting old to miss seeing a good-looking woman interested in him. "Not really."

"Do not lie to an old Cajun prosecutor, cherie."

"Well, come to think of it, she has suggested drinks, lunch…"

"Knowing little Miss 'My Family Came Over on the Boat After the Mayflower,' she has a lot more in mind than drinks or lunch."

"Amelie, I could almost be her grandfather."

"Trust me, cherie, she is not interested in serving you warm milk."

* * *

"Losing the ten or so pounds you've put on will help with the blood pressure," the doctor had told him.

There was no other reason to eat salad, Alexei decided. This was not a bad concoction, the dressing was well made, but it was salad. At least two-thirds rested in his stomach so he pushed it away and longed for a cup of coffee.

He looked up and saw Anne Hobard approaching his table. Shit. He thought he'd done a good job of avoiding her in the days since his conversation with Amelie.

"Good afternoon, Alexei. Mind if I join you?" Anne asked.

Alexei studied her. A body she kept in good shape in the World Court's fitness center, clothes from a top house in Paris, honey blonde hair, and a mouth more than kissable. Once, Alexei would have accepted a nooner on the desk in her office, but that hadn't interested him in a long time.

"Anne, court resumes in…"

She sat at the table, not across from him, but to his left. She scooted the chair closer to him. "We don't resume for a half-hour."

Alexei nodded, but picked up the depositions he'd been reading before she arrived.

"Are you feeling well?" Anne asked him. "I noticed you were rubbing your eyes. Do you have a headache? I have a great cure for that—I do a great neck massage."

"No, no headache. Old eyes."

"But nice ones."

Alexei ignored that and looked again at his papers.

"This trial has been harder than others. Harrowing," she said.

Without looking up, he said, "Yes."

"I don't usually go for the 'evil incarnate' line, but when I look at that bastard we're trying, I really do think evil walks around on two legs."

"More often than not, that's the case." His eyes never strayed from his reading.

"So, Alexei, I was wondering, well, I have two tickets to Ballet Russe in Amsterdam Saturday evening."

"How nice."

"I thought perhaps you might like to join me." When he said nothing, she continued, "Ballet Russe. You're Russian."

Alexei looked at her. "Do you like ballet?"

"I adore it."

"What are they performing?"

"I don't recall, but the reviews were excellent."

"Thank you, no."

"But why not?"

"It wouldn't be appropriate."

"We're colleagues, friends, but I don't work for you or you for me."

"That's not why it's inappropriate."

"The age difference doesn't bother me."

"Wrong again."

"Look, those tickets were hard to get. I had to pay a lot for them. I'm a public servant, like you."

"Anne, you have family money."

"Look, what's the harm? It'll relax you."

"Anne, I know the Director of Ballet Russe. He and I were in Komsomol together. The reviews weren't good, which he lamented when he and I had dinner the other night. Don't look so shocked. It wasn't even a hard ploy to see through."

"I don't know what you mean."

"Don't bother to bat your eyelashes. That's too much of a cliché. You know I'm married."

"She left you."

"No. I work here. She works elsewhere."

"That's not the story making the rounds."

"You listen to gossip too much for an intelligent woman."

"Well, that was defensive."

"So what if it were? Anne, even if I were separated from my wife, it wouldn't make me available."

"That same gossip said that doesn't usually matter to you."

"I'll give you that. One time it didn't. Now it does." Time to cut this off. "Let me make it clear to you. I have given you no indication I'd be interested in you other than in a professional capacity. You know that."

She leaned back in her chair, her face twisting in resentment. "Now's when you say, 'Anne, you're a damned fine lawyer.'"

"One of the best I've seen here. I've never seen anyone as self-assured as you in the courtroom. Your oral arguments are hard to rebut, your closing presentations eloquent and captivating, but when you get around me, you flit about like an airhead, which is a waste for a damned good lawyer."

"A damned good and lonely lawyer. As lonely as you."

Not in a million years, he thought. "Look, there are plenty of other men around here."

The resentment turned to spite. "You're giving me that line, too?"

"I can be harsher, Anne. I can be cruel, if that's what it takes."

She straightened and looked him in the eye. "Your wife isn't interested anymore. I am."

With a frisson of anger at Mai for putting him in this place, he said, "Anne, my wife and I do different work, work that keeps us apart. Unlike some men, I don't use that as an opportunity to fuck around. I'm not interested in replacing her in my bed, and I won't apologize for feeling that way."

"And, Mr. Hearts and Flowers, what will you do if she doesn't come back?"

"Go after her."

Anne Hobard stood up, knocking the chair over. Glad that looks didn't kill, Alexei watched her storm away. Amelie Richardson came to his side.

"Uh huh," she said. "I called that one, cherie, I did."

3

Sligo, Ireland

Mai kept her night-vision binoculars trained on T.J. Kennedy's public house while Munro tapped on the dashboard of their car, parked along the walkway beside the River Garavogue. The pub was on the other bank, and they had parked not far from the pedestrian bridge over the river.

Mai took the binoculars from her eyes. "Munro, your fidgeting is making me edgy."

His fingers didn't stop drumming. "It's good to have some edge before an op."

"That's true, but you're making me edgy enough I want to use the hypo on you and not Cill Chainnigh."

His fingers stopped drumming, and he folded his hands in his lap. "Sorry. I want to get on with this."

"We can't 'get on with' it until Cill Chainnigh actually gets here."

"I know, but who goes to a pub at one o'clock in the morning?"

"Irishmen."

They sat in silence, both sets of eyes on the pub and the streets leading up to it. Munro almost started the finger drumming again but stopped himself at a glare from her.

"So, I meant to ask," he said. "Why isn't your husband in on this?"

"He works at The Hague."

"I thought you'd been in the Balkans."

"I was until your summons."

"So, he wasn't in the Balkans with you?"

She glared again. "You want to discuss that now? Here?"

"Small talk keeps me from drumming my fingers and annoying you. What's up with you two?"

"We're in the middle of a row about work. He works where he wants to work, and I... Well, I'm sitting here in the cold in the dark in Sligo working on a private matter for you."

"He doesn't know you're doing this?"

"I don't need his permission, you know."

"Okay, easy. Where's the nephew?"

"I sent him back to Alexei. Besides, I have you here to protect me, since men seem to think I'm incapable of taking care of myself."

"Whoa. Guess I touched on a sore subject."

Mai returned the binoculars to her eyes. "It's a genius you are, Munro."

"Sorry. So much for small talk."

"I think I might prefer your drumming your fingers to your small talk topics."

"Okay, you pick the topic."

"All right, you said you'd never worked undercover, but you've done surveillance right?"

"Yeah, and we chatted away the whole time. Surely, you can multi-task?"

"Indeed, but a Land Rover with a plate matching what we got from MI-6 just pulled up outside T.J. Kennedy's.

Mai handed Munro the binoculars, and he saw a thick-set man emerge from the Land Rover's passenger side. The man leaned down and said something to the driver, then glanced around before he entered the pub. They both watched the Land Rover pull into a small car park a block away from the pub.

Mai slipped the binoculars into a backpack on the seat between them.

"Is it him?" Munro asked.

"It's Cill Chainnigh in the flesh. A lot of it."

"You're certain?"

"I'm certain. Are you ready?"

"I have been for days."

"All right, then, let's go."

Outside the car, Mai checked around them and led the way up the walkway to the bridge. Once on the other side, Mai wrapped her arm around Munro's waist, and his settled on her shoulders, their bodies touching from the hips upward. They staggered down the walk on the other side of the river, laughing and holding each other up. When they reached the Land Rover, Munro tapped on the glass. The driver lowered it and glared up at them, ear buds from a Walkman in his ears.

"Hey, buddy, hi," Munro said, his voice in a convincing slur. "I'm visiting here, and…"

"And I'm doing my best to improve Irish-American relations," Mai said, her hands wandering.

"Aye, I can see that," the driver said, with a touch of a smile. "Get on with ya, then."

"Look," Munro said. "We're really far from my hotel, and I was wondering if, you know, there's a place nearby."

"I said, move along." The driver wasn't amused anymore and started to raise the glass.

Munro took his wallet out. "I can make it worth your while."

Hidden by his wallet was a small aerosol can, which Munro sprayed in the driver's face. The driver got the door open, but Munro kept up the spray until the driver slumped to the side, held in place by the seatbelt.

"Easy, Munro," came Mai's whisper. "We only want him to look like he's sleeping off a drunk. Enough of that will make it a permanent nap."

She pushed the driver upright and released the seat belt. She handed Munro the driver's hat and began to pull off his coat. Munro shrugged out of his and donned the hat and coat. Mai got the driver into Munro's coat and buttoned it up. The two of them pulled the driver to his feet and drunk-walked him to a bench inside a bus shelter. Mai settled him there, Walkman in his pocket, music pouring into his sleeping ears.

Munro got behind the wheel of the Land Rover, and Mai stood beside the open door.

"How will we know when Kilkenny wants the driver?" Munro asked.

"Check the coat pockets for a cell phone."

Munro patted the pockets and held up a Nokia. "I don't know if my Irish accent will cut it."

Mai took the phone and thumbed through the Recent Calls list. "This looks like a throwaway. Only incoming calls."

"Kilkenny?"

"Most likely. If you see that number pop up, don't answer. Let Cill Chainnigh think the driver fell asleep. It'll be easier to take him if he comes to the car than directly in front of the pub."

"What if he hails a cab?" Mai looked around the empty streets and raised an eyebrow. "Yeah, right."

"All right, take a deep breath and try to relax. We have this under control."

"I'm not nervous. Impatient."

"Then, learn some patience as you sit in the nice, warm car while I skulk in the cold to wait for him to finish a pint or seven and decide to leave."

"Sorry about that."

"No, you're not, but you're forgiven. I'll be right over there behind that tree. When you get the call, tug on the brim of your cap, and I'll be ready."

* * *

Munro looked first at the dash clock then in the side mirror, adjusted so it showed him the door to the pub. The pub's dark façade was almost lost in the night, giving it an unsavory look. He turned his head toward where Mai had walked but couldn't see her.

Munro looked at the clock then at the side mirror, and kept that up for almost a half-hour.

When the phone rang, he jumped and looked again toward where Mai was supposed to be, hoping she hadn't seen that. The trilling stopped and started again a few seconds later. A check in the side mirror, and Munro saw Eamon Kilkenny pacing in front of the pub, phone to his ear. Munro tugged on his cap and slouched down in the car, pretending to sleep, one eye still on the side mirror. He saw Kilkenny pocket the cell phone and begin to waddle toward the Land Rover.

Munro stayed still when Kilkenny thumped on the window.

"All right, you lazy ass, wake up!" Kilkenny shouted.

Munro sat up and rolled down the window, and when Kilkenny saw the gun pointed at him, he smiled. "Where is she, then?"

"Behind you," Mai said.

Mai's arm went around Kilkenny's throat, and she jammed a syringe into the side of his neck, depressing the plunger. Munro stepped from the car and caught him as he slumped. Mai opened the rear door, and the two of them shoved Kilkenney inside. Munro stood there, staring at Kilkenny and pondering that this had all worked according to plan. Mai shoved the backpack into his hands.

"Get in back with him," she said. "There are plastic ties in there. Bind him hand and foot. Don't gag him, and turn his head so he doesn't choke on his own drool."

Munro didn't move.

"Munro. Hank, come on. We need to move. Get in the back and secure him."

"I'm wondering if I can stop myself from throttling him."

"Patience, remember."

Munro climbed in the back and shut the door while Mai got behind the wheel. Munro watched her check until she was satisfied no one had seen them, and he set to work.

* * *

Munro had lost track of how many hours he'd spent watching a naked, snoring Eamon Cill Chainnigh trussed to a chair in the safe house's kitchen.

"Linoleum floors clean up easier," Mai had said when Munro questioned the placement.

Cill Chainnigh showed no sign of waking, and Mai showed no sign of getting him to do so. Her pleas for patience be damned, Munro wanted something to happen.

He found Mai in the sitting room of the safe house. She had curled up on the window seat of the bay window, which showed the waters of Sligo Bay beyond, and, of all things, read a book. He stood where she couldn't help but see him and waited.

She turned a page with a rustle. Her eyes flickered over the pages, and she turned another.

Munro smacked the wall with a palm. "Dammit, Mai!"

"Sorry to read so loudly," she said, not looking up. When he didn't respond, she dog-eared a page and stood. "Now, the cliché is for you to say, 'How could you read a book at a time like this?'"

"Don't push me."

She laughed, and he didn't like it; but right now he needed her. She held the book out to him.

"If Frank McCourt got your daughter into her Irish roots, don't let her read any of this."

Munro took the book and looked at the cover: *Selected Poems of Seamus Heaney*.

"If she reads Heaney, she'll move here," Mai said.

Munro tossed the book onto a chair. "Another time. Let's get this fucking slow show on the road."

"You might have been born here, Munro, but you have no concept of what it is to be from here. I wasn't idly passing the time. I was refreshing myself on how people like Cill Chainnigh think."

"By reading poetry?"

She shrugged. "Irish poetry," she said, but his expression didn't relent. "All right, you're so eager, let's get started, shall we?"

Munro followed her to the kitchen, where she looked over Kilkenny's hunched body.

"At least he hasn't pissed himself like last night," she said. "Draw some cold water, and on my signal pour it over his head. I want you to stand off to one side, so I'm the first person he sees. And this is the protocol. I'm the interrogator. I'm the one who fulfills his needs and only the ones I decide. Got that?"

"I've had the training."

"Training and experiencing are two different things. The water, please."

Munro searched the cabinets until he found a large, plastic bowl, which he filled with cold tap water. After a nod from Mai, he dashed the water over Kilkenny's head and stepped back.

Kilkenny coughed and sputtered, but Mai stepped in and slapped his cheeks. "Look at me, Eamon. Look at me."

Kilkenny blinked water from his eyes and peered up at her.

Munro wanted to knock the smile from Kilkenny's face when he set eyes on Mai.

"Well, well, it's herself, then," the IRA man said. "You look good for a corpse, now, don't you? Much better than the people you betrayed. Bits and pieces they were. Tell me, did you fuck Declan the night before you killed him?"

"No, I did that the morning of."

Mai and Eamon had an exchange in Irish, far beyond Munro's tourist phrases of "please" and "thank you."

"Hey," he said. "English. I want to understand what you're saying."

Mai glared at Munro, and Kilkenny smiled when he heard Munro's voice.

"Ah, that would be the lovin' Da, wouldn't it?"

Kilkenny turned his head toward Munro, and Mai punched Kilkenny, hard, on the cheek and again up side his nose. Kilkenny's head snapped sideways, he shook his head, and he spat blood on the floor.

He looked at Munro again. "You're a policeman, lad. Are you going to let her beat me like that?"

"Eamon," Mai said, taking his chin and jerking his face back to hers. "We're not doing 'good cop, bad cop.' Don't look to him for help. You have his daughter, for Christ's sake. You need to worry about me."

"You're a slut, you know that, don't you?"

Mai landed the hardest blow Munro had ever seen a woman deliver in Kilkenny's gut, and they both had to step back as he spewed vomit. Mai was back on him with punches to his head, his gut, and back again. She stepped back, finally, shaking her right hand in pain. She went to the sink and ran cold water over her knuckles.

Munro went at her side. "What the fuck are you doing?" he whispered.

* * *

Mai shook her head as she let the cold water flow over her hand. "Why, I'm beating the crap out of the bastard who took your daughter. You want a turn?"

"We need to get him to talk, not beat him senseless."

"Munro, you asked for my help. Don't go prissy cop on me now. If you're thinking we can reason with him, you're wrong. He has no good side we can appeal to." She held her bruised knuckles under his nose. "This is the only thing he understands." She drew her Beretta. "This is another."

Gun still out, she went back to Cill Chainnigh. "All right, Eamon, I'm sure you've noticed, things aren't going the way you planned."

He grinned, teeth pink from blood. "Aren't they now?"

"I'll start by shooting off your toes, one by one. Then, I'll work my way up. Ankle. Kneecaps. Fingers, elbows."

"And spare me prick?"

Mai switched back to Irish. "I thought I'd leave that for the father of the girl you kidnapped."

Cill Chainnigh laughed. "You're a smart one, you are. You figured it out, didn't you?"

"Then, confirm it for me."

"And make it easy? Never."

"English, god damn it!" Munro said.

Mai turned an angry glare on him. "I will only warn you once. Shut up, and let me do what I have to do."

"I have a right to know what you're talking about, and there'll be no shooting."

Cill Chainnigh craned his head toward Munro again. "No stomach for it, do you, lad? You know she can beat me all she wants, and I won't talk." He turned back to Mai, speaking again in Irish. "I won't talk to you in time for you to save the girl, but I'll talk to him, after you finish it."

"Finish what?" she asked in English.

"You know what I'm talking about."

"Save me the trouble and the bullets and explain it."

"I won't talk because it doesn't matter what you do to me. I'm a dead man. Cancer. Four or five months to go, and that's longer than I was told to begin with."

"I figured that out, Eamon."

"Well, lass, I'm holding on until you die, but that innocent girl will die first, like your friends, like the man who loved you in Lifford. You can stop it right now. You die first, and I'll tell the man where his daughter is." His eyes went to her gun then back to her.

"Mai," Munro said, "we need to talk."

"Not now."

"Yes, now."

Cill Chainnigh laughed and shook his head. "Ah, poor man. He's worried about his daughter, he is, and you're not helping him out."

Mai put the barrel of the Beretta beneath Cill Chainnigh's chin.

"Mai! We talk now!" Munro said.

Mai gave him another withering look, holstered the Beretta, and strode from the kitchen to the sitting room, Munro at her heels. He closed the door on them.

"I think that's going well," Mai said.

"Mai, he wants you to kill yourself."

"Well, yes, that's obvious, Munro. When that doesn't work, he'll move on to his next ploy."

"Don't lose sight of what's at stake here."

"What am I losing sight of?"

"You're letting him bait you."

"Munro, I'm letting him think he's baiting me, and you're interfering. And, by the way, I'm not killing myself."

"You're playing a game with my daughter's life."

"It's not my game, Munro. It's Eamon's. He's playing with you, making you think my death will gain you Deidre's whereabouts. He's not going to tell us, no matter what I do to him or myself." She stepped close to him and took his hand. "Munro, I've held off telling you this because I needed your head in the game."

"What?"

"I'm sorry, Munro, but keeping your daughter alive was a liability for Cill Chainnigh. The longer he kept her, the more likely she'd be found.

Your daughter's probably dead, most likely since you told Cill Chainnigh we were on our way to Sligo. I'm sorry."

Munro's hand clenched hers like a vise. "Jesus, Jesus, no. You're wrong. You can't know that."

"I'm sorry. I truly am, and if this were someone other than your daughter, you would have realized it yourself."

"No, no. We have to get him to talk. We've got to give him something."

She pulled her hand from his grasp. "Well, I'm not giving him the satisfaction of blowing my brains out, or letting you do it for him."

"What?"

"That's his next try. If I won't do it, he'll work on you, tell you all you need to do is kill me and you get your daughter."

"I think I need for you to shut up, right now, and let me think."

Mai shook her head. "Think it through, out loud."

"He's a dying man. He'll let you beat him to a pulp, mutilate him, and he won't tell you. You know that, and now I know that."

"And?" she prompted.

"He doesn't know I know that."

"And that means we're still one up on him."

"All right, what now?"

"Now, it's time for 'good cop, bad cop.'"

4

Near Lifford, Republic of Ireland

Nicholai "Kolya" Antonov leaned against a tree and watched the dilapidated barn, as he had for more than an hour. No one came or went. He heard no sounds from inside and was convinced this was what his aunt had feared—the pursuit of a wild fowl.

Kolya's eyes strayed to a wide, mostly circular depression in the ground. Grown over in grass and other ground cover in the more than a decade since its creation, that had to be the crater left behind after *tetya* set off her bomb. He saw an overgrown hedge, the one where the SAS found her, bleeding from dozens of lacerations and half-dead. She had never told him the story, but *dyadya* had.

He checked his watch, the position of the sinking sun, and the barn again. When darkness edged in, he smiled. Light from a lamp shone through the holes in the barn. One day he would learn never to doubt his aunt.

Kolya picked up a duffle at his feet and crept toward the barn.

* * *

She'd given up weeping some time before. There were no more tears, and they made her feel weak, anyway. She tried to find a comfortable position, but her arms were pulled behind her, around a post, and tied at the wrist. Then, she remembered the suicide vest full of plastic explosive she wore and remained still.

Her guard sat on some old, old bales of hay, next to the lantern, and smoked. Not a safe thing to do, but neither was wearing a bomb. When he saw her looking at him, he leered, tongue licking his lips.

"I have to pee," Deidre Munro said.

"Hold it," the guard said and started to laugh. Her expression only egged him on. "So, what are you thinking, then? Are you trying to be brave, like your Da wants? Didn't he teach you how to get out of scrapes, then?"

Deidre lifted her head in defiance. "Sitting, tied up in a barn, wearing a bomb isn't something he planned for. Sorry."

"You've got spark left. I'll give you that."

"Well, when you put the bomb on me, I figured I'm dead any way."

The guard leered again. "Did you, now?"

"Yeah, an explosion will be quick. One second I'm alive, the next I'm dead. I can deal with that."

"Oh, that's not what worries you, is it? I've seen you cringe when I look at you. Aye, I've given it some thought. You're a nice enough piece, and it's a long time since I've had me a virgin."

Deidre laughed and got some satisfaction when the guard looked confused. "You'll be disappointed. I gave that up the night of Senior Prom. Rape is power, not sex, so you'll need to think of something else to rattle me."

The guard's smile left his face, and he gave her a hard stare through narrowed eyes. He took a final draw on the cigarette and made certain he dropped it on bare wood to grind it dead. With a glance at his watch, he came over to Deidre and knelt beside her. His fist in her hair, he pulled her head back, and kissed her, rough and sloppy. He lifted his face from hers and smiled.

"How's that, then, me darling?"

"God, Ronnie Hanson kissed better than that when we were twelve."

The guard slapped her on both cheeks. "Fecking little whore."

He did something to her vest, in the area where she'd seen the timer, then he pulled her coat closed over the bomb. He went back to the stack of bales and sat, lighting another cigarette.

"How long?" Deidre asked.

He grinned again. "Well, now, that needs to be a wee surprise, doesn't it?"

"Why aren't you leaving then?"

That damned smirk didn't leave his face. "I can spare you a few minutes, darlin'. Don't you worry."

"You're going to wait until the last minute, aren't you? So even if my Dad does get here, there won't be time to defuse it, disarm it, whatever."

The guard said nothing, only smoked and smiled.

"Look, please, don't do this to my Dad. He's a good guy. He didn't do anything to you or your people. I'll... I'll do whatever you want. Anything. Just take this thing off me, shut the timer off, something. Anything you want. I promise."

"Yeah, it's painful to lose a child. The Brits shot my baby brother. My Ma and Da never got over it. They're only in their fifties, but they look seventy."

"That's not my fault. It's not my Dad's fault. My Dad was born here. Don't do this to him, please."

"Sorry, lass. You've got three minutes to go. I couldn't stop it now if I wanted to, and I really don't want to."

Deidre couldn't stop a sob from escaping her throat. The guard laughed again; then, he stopped laughing, his face going slack. The cigarette slipped from his mouth to the floor. He lurched forward to his knees and fell face down on the barn's floor.

That was when Deidre saw the hilt of a large knife protruding from between his shoulder blades.

* * *

Kolya stepped into the halo of light from the lamp and crushed the smoldering cigarette. He knelt beside the dead man and pulled the knife free. He cleaned it on the man's coat and tucked it away in his boot.

When he neared the girl, he held up his hands and said, "Everything is okay now."

"Everything is not okay. Get this thing off me."

Kolya squatted by her and opened the coat. "Shh, shh. Patience." He looked over the bomb and shook his head. "Amateurs."

"God, who cares? Can you get this thing off me?"

"*Nyet*. No. If I move it, it explodes."

"Oh God! Oh God! Oh God!"

"Shh. Is all right. Is no problem."

"No fucking problem?"

"Look. Is all right."

She looked down at the timer. It had stopped at twenty-two seconds left. "But you said you couldn't..."

"I said we could not take off. I had to disarm first. It was amateur bomb. Easy to disarm. Now we can take off."

"Okay, now, I'm going to get hysterical."

"Let me get bomb off first."

Kolya cut the vest from Deidre Munro with the same knife he had used to kill her guard. Once he had it free, he held it at arm's length and walked with care to a far corner of the barn, where he tucked it behind more hay bales. He went back to Deidre and began to saw at the ropes on her wrists.

"Did my father send you?"

"No."

"Well, who are you?"

"I am nephew to a friend of your father's."

"The woman they talked about? Fisher?"

"*Da. Moya tetushka.*"

"What?"

"My aunt. There, you are free."

"I can't move my arms."

"Is circulation. Give them a moment." Kolya moved to sit beside her, took out his handkerchief, and began to clean her face.

"Where is my father?"

"In Sligo with my aunt. Is long story."

"Do you have a cell phone? Can I call him?"

"I have phone, but no coverage here. I want to get you away in case he has relief coming." He nodded toward the dead guard. "There. Face is clean. Better?"

"Yeah, thanks."

"How are arms?"

"Tingly, but I can feel them now."

"Okay, I have car parked in woods about one mile and a half from here. Can you walk?"

"Yes, but…" She bit her lower lip.

"What is it? Are you hurt somewhere?"

"No. I… I have to pee. Damn it."

Kolya stood and hauled her to her feet. "There is cow stall over there. Try to pee fast."

5

Sligo, Ireland

Munro winced when he and Mai reentered the kitchen and he saw the swelling of Kilkenny's face. The man had a coughing fit, and Munro went to the sink and drew a glass of water. When Mai walked behind Kilkenny, she smacked him on the side of the head.

Eamon Kilkenny laughed at that. "Ah, the return of your tender ministrations, Siobhan. I liked that name, Siobhan Dochartaigh. A sweet name, not like your English one."

"Who told you my real name?"

"Declan was in love with Siobhan Dochartaigh. Head over heels. He would have died for you, and he did, didn't he?"

"We're not talking anymore about Declan. Who told you my real name?"

Kilkenny turned his head to one side and spat. "I'll give you that one, I will."

"Go on, then. Tell me."

"An RUC constable's conscience got the best of him a few years back, and he decided he needed to do something for The Cause. He told me who you were. Told me all about how you pretended to be the real Siobhan."

"Did you kidnap his child as well?"

"Oh, not needed at all. He gave it up for free. Did you kill the real Siobhan, too?"

"His name."

"I gave you something. Now you give me something. What happened to sweet Siobhan Dochartaigh?"

"After she finished her gun-running sentence in America, she decided she didn't want to come back here. She's in Witness Protection, but not before she told me everything I needed to know to be her. What's the constable's name?"

"I killed him. I didn't want his conscience reversing on me."

"I'd rather confirm that myself. His name."

"Padraig O'Connor. You can go lay flowers on his grave. Your comrades at Lifford, we had to put them in one box, in one grave. There wasn't enough left to tell who was who. Your work, girl."

Munro stepped forward and held out the glass of water.

"Ah, is that for me, then? God, but me throat is dry," Eamon said.

"Munro, that is not for him," Mai said.

"How can the man talk, for God's sake, if we don't give him water?"

"How can you even think about the comfort of the man who kidnapped your daughter?"

"Hell, I'll give him my fucking house and pension if he'll tell me where she is."

"Well, now," Kilkenny said, "you sound like a man I can deal with. Not like the little whore here. Batting her eyes, getting us all to believe she was one of us, when all the while she was just another fecking traitor."

Fist raised, Mai stepped toward Kilkenny. Munro blocked her. "We agreed there'd be no more of that," he said.

"Then, your daughter's life is on you because I can get this piece of shite to talk."

"Whore," Kilkenny said. "Who paid you to kill your friends, the people who trusted you? How do you sleep at night, then, knowing you betrayed them, knowing you betrayed a man who loved you? How could you fuck him knowing you were going to kill him?"

Again her strength surprised Munro, as she pushed him aside and started to pound again on Kilkenny's face. Munro grabbed her by the waist and swung her aside, into the wall, a little harder than he intended, and he saw the expression on her face as she pushed off and swung her elbow into his chin. He backed away, dabbing at blood on his lip and thinking he might have deserved that.

Mai was punctuating her words to Kilkenny with her fists. "Tell. Me. Where. Deidre. Munro. Is."

Munro's arms encircled her, trapping hers, and pulled her away. Kilkenny spat out a bloody tooth, and gave her a smile. "Ah, thanks for that, darling. It's been a long time between boners."

Mai tried to lunge from Munro's hold, but he tightened it.

"That's it. You're done," he said. He frog-marched her down the hall and into the sitting room. He released her and raised his voice so Kilkenny could hear. "Come out of here, and I'll fucking kill you myself."

Mai gave him a smile and whispered, "It's up to you, now."

* * *

A weary Mai flopped into an armchair, and laid her head back. Eyes closed, she brought her breathing under control. Even then, the vibration of her cell phone jolted her.

"Yes?"

"Kolya here."

"Were you successful?"

"*Da*. She was exactly where you said. I have her in car. We are headed to rendezvous."

"Is she all right?"

"None worse for wear."

In the background, Mai heard someone she assumed was Deidre Munro say, "Is that my Dad? Can I talk to him?"

"Tell her he has unfinished business, but he'll be in touch shortly."

"What about loose end?" Kolya asked.

Mai looked toward the closed door. "Mr. Munro may be taking care of that."

* * *

Munro stepped around the spilled water and shards of the glass Mai had knocked from his hand earlier. He took another glass, filled it, and came up to Kilkenny. He held it to the man's swollen lips and let him drink.

"Ah, thank you, then, lad," Kilkenny said, his breath wheezing through what was probably a broken nose. "I need to tell you, so youse understand, this is nothing personal between you and me. I made sure no one touched your lass. She wasn't raped. You have my word."

"Your word?"

"Aye. I had to use someone to get to the bitch. It's just the way it is. No hard feelings."

Munro went back to the sink and set the empty glass in it. He took a chair, twin to the one Kilkenny sat in, and placed it back-first to the man. Munro straddled the chair and laid his arms atop the chair's back.

"Since that first phone call from you," Munro said, "all the aspects of Deidre's life have been passing before my eyes. Birthday parties. First Communion. School dances. Graduation. Waving to her as she went down the Jetway to fly here. And you think it's all right between us if you assure me she hasn't been raped?"

Kilkenny blinked at the coldness in Munro's voice. "Where's the bitch, then? This is between her and me."

"I've never experienced anything like this, like what's happened here. I've debriefed counterfeiters, the occasional nut job who threatened the President or First Lady. Those were always controlled situations. Lawyers present. All very civilized."

"Get her back in here, now."

"You don't make demands of me, you fucker. It's the other way around."

Munro leaned down and took a snub nose revolver from an ankle holster. He faced Kilkenny again.

"Mai's not coming back. Now, it's you and me."

"No deal, then, until you bring her back."

Munro thumbed the cylinder release on the revolver and pushed the cylinder clear of the frame. He depressed the plunger, and the five bullets fell into his palm. He reloaded one round and pocketed the others.

Kilkenny's eyes darted about—from the gun to the hallway to Munro's face and back to the gun. "Here, then, I said, no deal until I see her again."

Munro spun the cylinder and, without looking, pushed it back into the frame. He pointed the gun at Kilkenny's head.

"No, you're dealing with me, now. The father."

"You kill me, lad, you don't find your daughter."

"Tell me where she is."

"Not until the bitch is back in here."

"She's not a player anymore. You've got until the count of three."

"Now, it's a real cowboy you are, but you won't do it."

"One."

"You won't risk your daughter's life."

"Two."

Munro cocked the hammer, the click making Kilkenny twitch against his bindings.

"You're not like her, lad. She's the killer. She killed nine people in cold blood because a government paid her to. You love your daughter, but there's no love in that whore. You won't…"

"Three."

Munro pulled the trigger, but it fell on an empty chamber. Kilkenny flinched, and Munro glanced at the pool of urine spreading beneath the other man's chair.

"Let's see if you'll shit yourself this time."

"Hail Mary, full of grace…"

"One."

"The Lord is with thee. Blessed art thou among women…"

"Two."

"And blessed is the fruit of thy womb, Jesus. Holy Mary…"

"…Mother of God, pray for us sinners now and at the hour of our death," Munro finished for him.

On the word, "death," Munro pulled the trigger, and, again, it fell on an empty chamber.

"That's two down. Your odds aren't good, fucker. Are you a father?"

"No."

Munro cocked the gun again. "Then you don't know what a father will do to shield his child. One."

Kilkenny twitched so hard, the chair skittered an inch or two. "No, no, stop! I'll tell you. She's in Lifford. Where the bitch set off her bomb and killed my lads and lasses. What time is it?"

"Why?"

"She's strapped to a bomb. What time is it?"

Dread settling on him, Munro checked his watch. "Twenty after nine."

Eamon Kilkenny began to weep.

* * *

Mai rose when Munro came into the sitting room. He glanced around as if he'd never been here, as if she were a stranger. He lowered himself to sit on the sofa. She saw all the fragility there and knew she had to break her news with care, so he would believe her.

Munro spoke before she could. "She was where your bomb went off. Lifford. They wired her to a bomb. It went off twenty minutes ago. I loved her more than my life."

She walked to stand beside him. "Munro…"

He took her hands, pulled her down to straddle his lap. He mashed his mouth against hers, and his hands slipped under her sweater. Weeks since she'd been this close to a man, she didn't hesitate to open her mouth and didn't stop his hands, but she found her sense and pulled away. She took Munro's face in her hands.

"Munro…"

His voice thickened by desire, he said, "Liam. Call me Liam. My Irish name." He kissed her again, and this time her resolve was stronger.

Mai disengaged and pulled her mobile phone out. "There's someone you need to talk to."

Munro leaned back on the couch, his hands now at his sides. "Jesus, what's wrong with me. My daughter's dead, and I'm thinking with my dick."

Mai dialed a number and brought the phone to her ear. "It's called comfort sex, Munro, but you don't need it."

"What?"

Kolya answered, "*Da, da.*"

Mai held up a hand to quiet Munro. "Put her on," she told Kolya. She held the phone out to Munro. "It's for you."

"I don't understand…"

"Take the phone."

Munro put the phone to his ear. "Hello?"

"Daddy?"

Mai rose from Munro's lap and gave him privacy.

* * *

Mai studied Eamon Cill Chainnigh. You needed no special training to know a neck bent at that angle was fatal. Munro hadn't been schooled in the proper way to break a neck, the quick way. Cill Chainnigh had struggled, but Munro had prevailed.

Despite Cill Chainnigh's corpulence, he seemed small, and she realized that's what he was, all he ever had been. A man small in his politics and in his morals.

Seeing him dead, something lifted, something she'd carried a long time, and she felt nine people rested easier in their single grave now. Not exactly what she'd promised MI-6, but sometimes these things happen.

And she gave a brief thought to Declan, sweet Declan, who had loved her before she killed him.

She gave Cill Chainnigh not another glance and decided Munro had had plenty of time for his call.

When she re-entered the sitting room, Munro had stood up from the sofa. He turned slightly from her and swiped at the tears she'd seen on his face.

"She's okay," he said, his tone still showing his surprise.

"I'm glad."

"About what just happened…"

"Don't you dare apologize. Collect your things and let's head to the van."

"What about…"

"It's MI-6's job to clean up. Let's go see your daughter."

6

Mai busied herself making tea and letting a bottle of red wine breathe on the kitchen table. She glanced up and out the window and spotted Kolya on patrol. He saw her and waved. She told herself not to debate what she was about to do, and she didn't. She picked up her mobile phone and dialed a long distance number. After three rings she heard the voice she would know anywhere.

"Bukharin here. I am unable to take your call. Please leave a number for a return call."

That was Alexei. Short, sweet, to the point. Mai heard the beep but hesitated.

"Hi, it's me. Well, I'm sure you know that, and, well, where are you that you're not answering your phone at dawn?" Disappointment fed her anger. "Didn't you make it home last night? It didn't take long to replace me."

She hung up, regretted what she'd said, and started to redial. Munro entered, and she put the phone away. "How is she doing?" Mai asked.

"The hot bath did wonders. Sleep will do more, which is what she's doing right now." Munro looked at the tea implements and the bottle of wine. "Tea and wine?"

"Tea is the British cure-all. Wine, the French. I'm having tea. What can I pour for you?"

"Hell, it's evening somewhere. Wine."

Mai fixed her tea, poured Munro a glass of wine, and sat at the long side of the table. Munro sat in the chair next to hers and leaned a tad against her.

"Did Deidre have any injuries?" she asked.

"Bruising. Nothing serious. No, uh, rape."

"That's a relief. Usually it's a given. I'm glad Eamon's agenda was elsewhere."

"Speaking of agendas, I've been thinking," Munro said.

"I noticed you were quiet on the flight here."

"I think you figured this all out a long time ago."

"Why would you think that?"

"The Russian guy was in the right place."

"Are you complaining about the outcome?"

"No, but I am wondering if my daughter and I have been used."

"You were, she was, by a terrorist."

"That much is obvious. What about you? How did you use us?"

Mai showed him her pique. "My 'Russian' saved your daughter's life, I let you have a free snog and grope, and you sit here in my kitchen, in my house, asking me if I wanted Eamon Cill Chainnigh bad enough to take advantage of your situation."

"Yes, and you kissed back."

"I never turn down a good snog, Munro, and I'm a user. It's a valuable asset in my business."

"And everyone you meet along the way, we're just pawns, right? Means to an end?"

"Sometimes, but I don't casually toy with people's lives for selfish purposes."

"Yeah, I'm sure altruism is high on your list of priorities. So, when did you figure it out?"

"Munro, why is that important?"

"Because I don't think I can move on without knowing."

"You do know some things are best staying unknown? We beat Cill Chainnigh at his own game. That's all that matters."

"To you, maybe. When did you know?"

Mai drank some tea and looked him in the eye. "In the lounge of the Hay-Adams."

She expected to get the remainder of the glass of red wine in her face, and she saw more than betrayal pass over his face.

"Fuck you."

"You did have that in mind a few hours ago. Look, Munro, I knew Cill Chainnigh, and as soon as you told me your story, I knew what he was after."

"But how could you know where?"

"Lifford is a low point in IRA history. It's symbolic. I guessed he would take your daughter to the scene of my 'crime.' When the bomb she wore went off, I'd be killing her by proxy where I killed before."

"We could have gone there when we first got to Ireland."

"No, that was exactly what we couldn't do. Cill Chainnigh would have guessed that and probably didn't put her there until the last minute." She anticipated his next question. "I couldn't tell you because you wouldn't have kept your head about you."

"You used us."

"I understand how you may think that, but you're reacting as a father, not as a tactician. If we'd moved in too early, they would have killed her."

"You can't know that."

She smiled and laid her hand on his arm. "You think entirely too highly of me. I knew it because if the situation were reversed and I had to use something or someone to get to Cill Chainnigh, I would have. I would have done the same thing he did."

"Jesus…"

"Munro, I was trained by a former KGB agent. Threatening someone's family is far more effective than physical violence. Cill Chainnigh thought the same way."

"What you knew was her life was in the balance, and you went ahead with your revenge."

Anger rose up in her again. Ungrateful git. "Kolya was on scene. He wasn't going to let anything happen to your daughter."

"You used me, you used her, to get back at an old enemy."

"Why does that surprise you? I'm a spy. I manipulate people on a daily basis sometimes for vague agendas called peace and national security."

"And you're always there to save the day."

"Most of the time. This I had under control from the beginning, and your daughter lies sleeping upstairs instead of dead in a shallow grave no one would ever find. You get to take her home, and I was able to give that to you. I'm glad I was."

"All that sweet talk is just more manipulation."

"Munro, you came to me, remember?"

"What choice did I have?"

"Not much. Look, if you want to be angry with me for the methodology, I respect you for that."

"You respect me?"

"I let you snog and…"

"Yes, yes, I remember." He smiled at her. "I won't forget it for a while."

She decided that Munro must not get kissed very often. They sat in quiet for a while, and she saw Kolya go by the window again. One last loose end.

"Munro, you killed Eamon Cill Chainnigh."

Munro shrugged and drank some wine. "Maybe he died from your beating."

"That was good, but you don't quite lie well enough to be a spy."

"Lying? Me? You're mistaken."

"My beating didn't break his neck."

"He kidnapped my daughter."

"But this was my revenge?"

"Okay, bad choice of words. Personally, I think justice was well-served."

"Munro, you're a good cop. You would never have killed Cill Chainnigh for personal revenge. So why?"

"I figured you were going to anyway."

"Actually, I was going to turn him over to MI-6."

"Oh, I almost believed that."

"Yeah, I'll work on it."

This time, he lay an arm around the back of her chair, his hand resting on her shoulder. "From what he told me, from what you told me, I didn't want you to have another death on your conscience."

The altruism he'd accused her of not having surprised her in him. "God, Munro, surely you know I don't have one of those any longer."

"I don't believe that."

"Believe what you want, but don't ever patronize me."

Her tone moved his arm from her chair, and he got up and walked to the counter to pour himself more wine.

Glass in hand, he turned back to her and leaned against the counter. "What about the other thing?"

"What other thing?"

"The kissing, groping thing, and you did that on purpose to make me say it again, didn't you?"

"Perhaps I did. It was an emotionally charged moment."

"So, it was nothing."

"I didn't say that, but it has to be nothing."

"No, it doesn't."

"Yes, it does, and I thank you for it."

He gave her a frown. "It has to be nothing, but you're thanking me for it?"

"That showed me being with my husband isn't as difficult as I've told myself it is. You and Deidre can stay here and rest as long as you want, but tomorrow morning I'm going to The Hague and hope Alexei hasn't moved on."

"He hasn't."

"You don't even know the man."

"True, but I know I wouldn't."

She came to the sink to put down her mug, and Munro cupped her cheek.

"Thank you for my daughter's life."

Mai nodded, and Munro turned to go. "Munro?"

He turned back to her.

"You do realize I'll call your marker in at some point?"

Munro smiled his charming smile at her, one that made her wonder how it would have been to let him have his comfort sex.

"Why, I believe you said I'm a useful ally to have watching your back, and you look forward to working with me again someday."

"Of course, that's exactly what I meant."

7

Outside The Hague, Netherlands

Grocery bags in one arm, Alexei entered the side door of his rented beach house, per Dutch custom. His two companions pulled onto the parking pad behind his car, and he left the door open for Amelie and Joseph Richardson. He began to put away his purchases and listened to their banter as they made their way into the house.

"No, sir, there is no way a Russian is going to cook a Cajun dish better than my husband."

Alexei heard the smack of a kiss on a cheek. "Thank you, Baby," came Joseph Richardson's bass.

"Thank me later, Baby."

"Oh, yes, indeed."

By now they were in the kitchen, and Joseph went to embrace her. Though he didn't let them know he saw, Amelia nudged her husband away with a nod toward Alexei. Displays of affection didn't upset him. They did, however, remind him of what he no longer had.

"Hey, Alexei," Joseph said. "You sure you don't want my help with that etouffe?"

"I'm sure, Joe. I think you might be pleasantly surprised by my effort. You can select some wine from the rack and open it to breathe."

"Wine coming up."

"Alexei," Amelie said, her voice soothing. "There's a message light on your phone."

"What about it?"

"You've got a message."

Alexei stopped unpacking the groceries and looked at the phone's blinking light. He went back to his task.

"Aren't you going to listen to it?" Amelie asked.

"No. It's probably Anne Hobard."

"Or it's Mai."

"She'd call the office. She doesn't have this number."

"Actually, she does."

"How?"

"Well, I sent it to her."

"When?"

"A few weeks ago. Look, hold off interrogating me and play the message."

"I'll do it later. Dinner is the priority now."

"Pride goeth before the fall, Alexei."

Alexei strode to the phone and pushed the "play" button. Mai's voice filled the room.

"Hi, it's me. Well, I'm sure you know that, and, well, where are you that you're not answering your phone at dawn? Didn't you make it home last night? It didn't take long to replace me."

"Well, damn," Amelie said.

"Yes, thank you for that, Amelie."

"Call her back."

"And react to her tantrum? No."

Joseph re-entered with two bottles of wine in hand. "How did a Commie get such good taste in wine? I'm looking forward to this as much as the food. Ami, Baby, I think I left my blood pressure pills in the car. Will you go check for me?" He gave her a wink.

"Sure thing, Sugar. Don't drink all that wine before I get back."

"I suppose you heard?" Alexei asked.

"Yes, man, I did. Ami's right. Call your wife. Reassure her. Don't both of you be stubborn. That'll only end badly. It almost did for Ami and me when we were young and neither of us would give."

"It's more complicated…"

"Son, no, it isn't, if you love her. Call her."

He wondered why he hadn't done that in the first place. No, he knew. "Excuse me a moment," he said.

Alexei went into his bedroom, trying not to remember it had been two decades since he'd slept alone every night. He took out his cell phone and dialed not his wife, but his nephew.

"*Da, da,*" Kolya said.

"Are you with Mai?"

"Where else would I be? Where are you, *Dyadya?*"

"In The Hague. Where are you?"

"We are in Belfast, Ireland. It is shithole."

"That's one way to describe it. Why are you there?"

"Directorate recalled Mai from Bosnia at request of Secret Service, but it was personal matter. A kidnapping."

"What? Whose kidnapping?"

"Is long and complicated story."

"Start at the beginning."

* * *

Amelia and Joseph were most of the way through a bottle of wine when Alexei emerged from his bedroom, overnight bag in hand.

"Is everything all right?" Amelie asked.

"I'll know in a few hours. I mean, she's all right, but it's time the two of us had a talk."

Amelie raised her eyes heavenward. "Hallelujia!"

"You're welcome to the food, but, Joe, you'll get to do the cooking after all. I hope to get a plane out of Schipol this evening."

"No need. While I was out 'looking for' Joe's pills, I made a few calls. The Tribunal's jet is waiting for you."

"Amelie, I couldn't…"

"I'm the Chief Judge, and if I say it's allowed, it's allowed. As far as I'm concerned it's a professional matter. No one wants to see you moping around anymore. Well, except maybe Anne Hobard."

"I don't think moping is…"

"Get going. I'm a hopeless romantic. Don't disappoint me."

8

Belfast, Northern Ireland

Kolya Antonov wished for a cigarette then remembered even if he had one he couldn't smoke it around his aunt. He leaned against a window sill and watched the driveway to the house on the edge of the city. After a moment, he saw headlights and waited to make certain it was a taxi, then he headed for the front door before his uncle could knock and wake the house.

Alexei raised an eyebrow when Kolya caught him with his fist in the air. Kolya laid his finger on his lips. Alexei stepped inside for Kolya to close the door, and uncle and nephew greeted each other with hugs and kisses on each cheek.

"Is she asleep?" Alexei asked.

"Finally. I don't think she had for two or three days."

"Some things never change. What about you?"

"Ah, I have stamina. Now you are here, I will sleep."

"Are Munro and his daughter still here?"

"*Da, da.* Mai will let them go home tomorrow on her jet."

"Was Mai in Lifford?"

"*Nyet.* She was in Sligo, but old demons…" Kolya paused and shrugged.

Alexei glanced up the stairs then back to his nephew. "I think I'll have a talk with Mr. Munro about all this."

"But that can wait until morning."

Alexei gave him a smile. "Yes, it can. Wish me luck."

"*Udachi.*"

Though it had been several years since he'd been in this house, Alexei remembered how to tread the stairs to keep them from creaking. The same with the trek down the long hallway. He tried the door and found it unlocked. Fighting down nervousness, he eased it open and stepped inside.

She had left the curtains open, and the moonlight showed her the way he'd seen her hundreds, thousands of times—curled up on her side, clutching a pillow. He smiled at that and at the fact the moon was bright enough to show one hand slipping beneath the pillow her head rested on.

"No guns, please," he said. "It's me."

Mai sat up and turned on the bedside light. Even with the bed-head and the dark circles showing how little sleep she'd gotten, his whole body reacted to the sight of her.

"Well, Kolya's fired," she said.

"Actually, he let me in."

"What are you doing here? How did you know where I was?"

"I got your phone message."

He saw the moue of embarrassment. "I was going to call you back and tell you to disregard. I was pretty tired at the time."

"It's all right. Amelie needed an early conference before court. That's why I wasn't home when you called."

"You don't have to tell me something I should have known. That doesn't explain how you knew where I was."

"I called Kolya a few hours ago to see what was going on."

"And he said nothing at dinner. Now I understand that little smile he had."

"He'd rather not displease you. You pay him too well."

"Obviously, I pay him too much."

He knew better than to expect her to make the first move, so he walked to the bed and sat down beside her. She didn't move away when he laid a hand on her knee.

"Hi," he said.

"Hi, yourself."

"Anything interesting happen lately?"

"You might say that."

"Care to share?"

Her movement fluid, she gathered her legs under her and leaned forward into his arms.

"Do you really want to talk?"

Alexei turned off the light.

DAYS OF AULD LANG SYNE

1

December 29, 1999
Washington, D.C.

Wiliam Henry Munro felt as if he had a ton of grit beneath his eyelids. The late nights he'd been keeping weren't good for his efficiency. He needed to be alert, but last minute details or changes to the schedule kept him awake at night and in the office.

His office, in this case, was a temporary command center erected on the National Mall. At a glance, you'd call it a tent, but it was a tent with rooms and constructed of a special material that shielded spoken and electronic communications from eavesdroppers.

Eavesdropping was the least of Munro's worries. The safety of tens of thousands of average citizens and hundreds of VIP's, muddled by the overlapping jurisdictions of more than a dozen Federal and local law enforcement agencies, were the concerns that had dogged him day and night for weeks. The cause of all this concern was a non-entity at least, a marketing scam at most.

By his own reasoning—and he'd been good at science—the real millennium was a year away. Munro supposed that, despite the popular cult science fiction movie 2001, that wasn't as sexy or marketable as "Y2K" or "MM." If you weren't Christian, it wasn't the millennium either, just another year.

Add in a good dose of paranoia about what would happen to some aged computers when their internal clocks clicked over to a year ending in "00" and vague threats of internal and external terrorism, Munro would be happy if the whole "America's Millennium" thing—the three-hour entertainment extravaganza and fireworks display on the Mall—were called off. In that respect, Munro admired the mayor of Seattle, Washington. After several arrests of Arabs with fake passports and bomb-making ingredients in their cars as they attempted to come in from Canada, the Seattle mayor had canceled the city's official celebration at the Space Needle.

Why the Mayor of D.C. or the President didn't do the same, was a question Munro asked in silence. As head of security for the event, it was his job to make certain no one got hurt. Questioning the decisions of bureaucrats and politicians was something he didn't do.

When the planning had begun, the FBI—of course—had lobbied hard to get the top slot, but the presence of the First Family at the event gave the ball to the Secret Service. And Munro could only blame himself—do a good job for the President and he recommends you for special events. His supervisor had agreed Munro's seniority and his demonstrated abilities made him the best choice. Munro accepted it because it was his swan song. After twenty-five years of serving five different presidents, Munro would retire when the new year rang in.

Any other prospective retiree might have accepted this challenge with a FIGMO mentality—fuck it, got my orders. Not Munro. He approached it with his usual thoroughness and attention to detail. He had smoothed the FBI's ruffled feathers by putting several of their agents in key organizational positions. He made certain the Capitol Police were involved, and he found roles for the BATF, Customs, DEA, Park Police, MPDC, and more. And he'd learned there was a D.C. Public Housing Police—who knew? He made a place for them as well.

The only thorn in his side was that most of the agents assigned to him were young enough to be his children, among them several women Munro would have considered asking out once he retired. They managed to quell that ardor by calling him "Sir."

One such woman spoke to him now, giving the hourly update on street closings. She was dressed in tactical black BDUs and body armor, but Munro wasn't so old he couldn't see the nice figure beneath it. Then, he sighed softly. He felt like a dirty old man lusting after one of his subordinates. He made certain he kept a professional demeanor, but that didn't keep him from flushing at his thoughts. He'd worked with a lot of women in his career and never wanted to be considered anything except safe.

Ah well, in three more days maybe I'll cut loose, he thought. Then, he smiled when he knew that wouldn't happen.

The agent finished her report, and he thanked her, tossing a "good job" as she walked away and while he watched her backside. He checked his watch, wondering if he could get in a nap before the next principals' briefing. When he saw the time he wondered if U.N. representatives were always late or was it this particular one?

"She was rather attractive, wasn't she?"

Munro smiled and wondered if mind-reading was one of Mai Fisher's talents. He turned to greet her. All thoughts of younger women left his head.

She looked rested, relaxed, dark eyes luminous, dark hair in a severe French braid. She had dressed in what passed for the U.N. Security Force's utility uniform—dark blue commando sweater, dark blue pants tucked into Lady Magnum combat boots. She wore her body armor under her sweater, and the ubiquitous Beretta was holstered at her right hip. Insignia on her turtleneck bore the initials "UNSF," and the epaulets at her shoulders showed a colonel's rank.

God, he was glad to see her.

"Don't you do anything the usual way?" he asked.

"The usual way is boring." She pointed to the ID badge clipped to her gun belt. "I did check in and get the appropriate identification, though I saw at least three ways I could get around your security."

Munro felt his defenses come up before he remembered she liked to pull chains.

"I hear you got a new job," he said.

She shrugged, and he thought he saw some emotion in her eyes. "Well, yes. It keeps me from being the idle rich."

"Chief of Security for the War Crimes Tribunal. That's quite a cherry job. You made it sound like nothing much."

"Compared to what I used to do, it is nothing much, but I'm with Alexei. And that's important to me."

"You miss the old life?"

"Let's see. Do I miss skulking about, eavesdropping on people, roughing up bad guys, getting slapped around, shot at, followed, threatened? You bet your ass I do. We get an occasional spike of intrigue at The Hague, but mostly it's gossip. Who's fucking whom, that sort of thing."

"Do I detect some bitterness?"

The look she gave him made him drop the question.

He pointed to an epaulet. "Do I have to call you Colonel Fisher?"

"You do, and I'll shoot you. The rank came with the job. Alexei says it gives me credibility, but there was a reason I didn't stay in the British Army. So, your message said you needed my help. Official, this time."

"Yes, it was. The request specified your arrival two days ago."

"You know I rarely jump at the command of the U.S. government, but I'm here now. What's the threat you need my help with?"

"We've downplayed it, kept it only among a close group of need-to-know folks, but we believe it's a credible threat from a white supremacist group. Their message indicated they'd be coming to the Mall to kill all interracial couples."

All joking left her face. "You have a name for this organization?"

"New Patriot City."

Munro thought Mai Fisher might have paled, but he decided it was the artificial lighting. She stepped closer to him and lowered her voice.

"It's not Patriot City's prophet Elijah. He's dead."

"That was the Christian Identity preacher from the Kansas City thing?"

Her indication of surprise was a raised eyebrow.

"When I put in the request through your Mr. Nelson, he sent someone to brief me. Oh, and the threat came from a woman, not a man."

"Unusual. Patriot City didn't believe in putting women in places of authority. How did she make contact?"

"A letter to me."

"Why you?"

"My position as coordinator was announced in the media."

"Do you still have the letter?"

"We dusted it for fingerprints. None. Not even a partial."

"I want to read it."

"I have a copy here…"

"No. I want to read the original and see the envelope. What was the postmark?"

"Idaho."

"No surprise there. How did you know it was a woman?"

"She signed the letter, 'Sarai, Aryan Mother.'"

She considered what he'd told her. That shadow of emotion crossed her face again, but she recovered.

"I still find it interesting it's a woman," she said. "Elijah had a distinct opinion of the role of women, and heading up a New Patriot City was not one of them. You know, you really need Alexei here. He was the one undercover in the original Patriot City."

"He didn't come with you?"

She gave him a coy smile, something he wouldn't have expected from her. "What's wrong, Munro? Afraid you won't have me all to yourself?"

"Well, not exactly."

"Alexei is still in The Hague, noting the fact that the request was only for me."

"How much did you tell him about, you know?"

"You mean, did I tell him about the snogging? No, I decided that was best between us. How is Deidre, by the way?"

He smiled at her. "She's great. Spent most of the last year in counseling, but she's back studying at Trinity. She's a lot more careful now, though."

"Good, I'm glad she's all right. I hear you're retiring."

He wondered how she would know that but realized finding that out wouldn't be difficult for a spy. "Right after this is all over."

"Are you headed for Fiji or Tahiti or some such, or do you want a job?"

"A job? With you?"

"So you could tempt me every day? No. I own a private security business that's expanding. It could use someone with your experience."

"Well, I hadn't given much thought to what comes next."

"Why leave, then?"

"Oh, it's time. When I start thinking of my agents as my children, it's time for new blood."

"I'll send you some information about the company, and you can contact me with any questions. You'll have to pass the entrance tests and the interview on your own. Okay, enough small talk. Let's get back to this threatening letter from New Patriot City. I've not kept up with America's rightwing nut jobs recently, but I can get Directorate analysts to do some digging and get current intelligence."

"Intelligence? We've already confirmed the existence of a group calling itself New Patriot City."

"Don't be defensive. Patriot City has become a legend among extremist groups since it came down. Any half-assed group could call itself New Patriot City. That doesn't mean it has access to the network Patriot City set up across the country."

"Our intelligence indicates it's the real thing."

"Oh, let me guess—your Fibbie brothers in arms assured you of this, right?"

"Yeah. Something called Project Meggido..."

"Plagiarized from a report I did back in 1995. I suppose I could sue, but there's that covert status thing. Allow me the comfort level of having my organization verify it. Am I going to be able to see that letter?"

"Sure. It's in an evidence locker at Secret Service headquarters, but I can have it here within the hour."

"Good. Thanks. I assume there's a secure line here somewhere?"

She gifted him with a smile, and he basked in it.

"Sure. I'll show you."

"I'll call the Directorate and get them moving on this. When's your next principals briefing?"

"Two hours."

"Let's get moving."

* * *

After finishing her official calls, Mai leaned back in the chair and glanced around the secure communications cubicle, marveling at the technology that made cloth resistant to electronic eavesdropping.

The curtains surrounding her were as dark as her mood. Nearly five years behind her, America's penchant for right-wing loonies was something she thought never to involve herself in again. Someone had other plans, apparently.

She took out her satellite mobile phone, glad she was enclosed since it was a classified, Directorate prototype, and placed a call to a private number in The Hague. A sleepy voice answered, and she indulged herself by imagining Alexei naked.

"I understand your wife was out of town, so I thought I'd call," she said.

"She's away, but she has spies everywhere," Alexei said.

"And she knows your every move."

"Were the Feds happy to see you?"

"Munro was. I faxed you a threat letter from a woman who calls herself Sarai. She claims to be from New Patriot City."

"Shit!" She heard him mutter other curses in Russian. "I'm putting you on hold. Let me get to the fax." In a few minutes, he picked up the phone. "Yeah, I got the fax."

"Anything familiar?"

"The name Sarai rings a bell. I think she was one of Elijah's harem, but I don't think I ever spoke to her. I believe Karen said she was one of Elijah's regulars and had a child of his. This letter is pretty standard Patriot City crap. Have our analysts verified it?"

"Yes."

"Any sightings yet?"

"Analysis is working on it. The Metro area has added a lot of surveillance cameras for this millennium event, and it's a lot to go through. Do you think she's a true believer?"

"I can't judge that since I don't know much about her, but I do remember Karen telling me that Elijah's women were some of the most zealous adherents of his philosophy."

"Would she be a shooter?"

"The women got basic firearms training. Nothing tactical. Just defense. Has the Secret Service done any projections on how many interracial couples could be attending this thing?"

"Not that I know of, but that's pretty impossible to predict, given the diversity and general attitude of tolerance in this area. I'm sure there are a lot of couples of all types."

"True, but she'll be interested only in black-white couples."

"That could still be hundreds, Alexei. Is it possible she's part of a hit squad or a loner?"

"Could be either. I'm sorry I can't tell you more. I've purposely not kept up with this. Do you have an ID yet on this woman, other than Sarai?"

"Not yet. Our analysts are working on it. If she hasn't committed any crimes, getting an ID in time will be difficult."

"Did you get the Biblical reference?" Alexei asked her.

"I think so. Sarai was Abraham's wife. She was barren and gave Abraham one of her handmaidens, who had a child. Sarai then had a child and had the handmaiden and her child exiled. What? Do you think that's relevant?"

"I'm not sure…"

He didn't speak for several moments, and she tried to keep her impatience at bay.

"What is it?"

"I'm trying to recall something Karen told me about a woman Elijah kicked out of Patriot City."

Mai gritted her teeth at the third mention of the name, Karen, an ATF agent also undercover in Patriot City when Alexei went there. While there, Karen and Alexei had a brief affair—to maintain cover was Alexei's excuse. Typical Alexei. Because he'd moved on, he assumed Mai had as well. One more mention of that name, though, and Mai wasn't going to let it pass.

"Yes," he said. "I remember. A woman who had one of Elijah's oldest children had a girl, and this Sarai, much younger, had a boy. Sarai managed to get the older woman out of favor with Elijah, and he kicked her out. She settled in Missouri near Patriot City because Elijah managed to find a sympathetic judge to give him joint custody."

"That woman would be able to give us a name. That's a great lead, Alexei."

"It's not much to go on because I don't have the other woman's name."

"It's a start and more than what I had before. I'll pass it along to the analysts. Sorry to wake you so early."

"No problem. It's good to hear your voice. Why did you wait two days to fax this to me?"

"I just got it today."

"The Feds sat on it?"

"No. I made a side trip and arrived on-scene here today. I was going to tell you when I got back."

She hoped that would put off a long-distance argument. No such luck.

"Why do you let him pull your chain? He whines about the injustice of it all, and you respond. John Carroll is where he belongs, and he will get the justice he deserves. When will you see he's the coward who keeps putting you on a guilt trip? He's not in prison because of something you didn't do. He's there because he killed nearly 200 people."

"Well, then, it was wonderful talking to you as always. I'll check back if the lead you gave me produces anything."

"Go ahead, cut me off when you know I'm right."

"I'm burning satellite time, and I didn't call to be reminded over and over again about your lover Karen or about my part in putting Carroll in prison."

"Karen was not my lover."

"What else do you call someone you sleep with? This conversation is over, Alexei. I'll talk to you later."

Mai ended the call and turned off the satellite phone so all he'd get was voice mail. A headache started to pound behind her eyes, fueled by jet lag, frustration, and anger—anger at herself, anger at Alexei for being right.

He was the second man important to her she'd displeased in the past two days.

2

Two Days Earlier
Terre Haute, Indiana

John Thomas Carroll's jailhouse pallor was unchanged from when she had visited him in Supermax, the federal prison in Colorado. His face was fleshier, his frame more filled out—the result of little exercise and starchy prison food. The routine in Terre Haute differed little from that in Supermax—twenty-three hours a day in a six-foot by twelve-foot cell, one hour a day for "recreation" in another room with half a dozen armed guards.

At Supermax he could converse with two other inmates, both convicted bombers as well. After his transfer to Terre Haute, since Supermax didn't do executions, his conversations were with his lawyers, the guards, his family on a rare visit, or Mai Fisher. And this was her first visit in more than a year.

Their acquaintance spanned just six years, and he'd been behind bars most of that time. Now, some maturity and the extra weight gave him presence and confidence—or was it arrogance? He was a man in his early thirties who wasn't likely to see forty, a stage where adulthood showed in the face and body language.

When he entered the visiting room, he was in the standard shackles, but this time wore a stun belt. One guard, who would remain in the room with them, held the control. Mai had observed this over CCT as she stood with the warden, and she complained about the belt.

"Standard procedure for dangerous inmates," was his reply.

"You know his record. He's made no trouble from the time he was taken into custody to now. He's no threat to me. Take it off him, or I'll make certain the U.N. Human Rights Council inspects this prison from ceiling to basement and releases its findings in an open session of the Security Council."

The bluff worked. The guard removed the belt, but the shackles had to stay. And they got privacy to talk—as much privacy as you could have with guards watching your every move through the window in the door and by surveillance camera.

"You've put on some weight," she said, when he greeted her with indifference.

"Yeah," he said, with a smirk. "Maybe I'll get so fat the drug dosage won't be enough."

Gallows humor—or more appropriately, lethal injection humor. She ignored it. "How are your family?"

The smile left his face, and he shrugged. "The same. My mother said it upsets her too much to see me here, so she's not coming anymore. Big surprise."

"It probably does upset her."

"No, it's a convenient excuse for her. My Dad is glad I'm closer now, but he doesn't drive long trips very often, and my sister..." He broke off with a shrug to cover the emotion in his eyes. "She's too busy getting on with her life, and I haven't seen you in more than a year."

"We talked about that. When I come, it takes a visitor slot away from your family."

"Another excuse. What's the real reason you haven't come?"

"I have a job, one that's not easy to get away from," she said.

"Out spying on more people?" After her silence, he leaned toward her, smiling. "Really, who am I going to tell?"

He had a point. "In the Balkans for a while." She saw that piqued his interest.

"Where?"

"Kosovo."

"During the bombing?"

"Before and after."

"See any action?"

"A little. Mostly I saw man's inhumanity to men, and women, and children."

"So, you supported the bombing?"

"I wanted something simpler, though not very viable." She smiled and said, "A 'private' conference with Slobodan Milosevic."

He laughed at that. "Somehow I think old Slobo wouldn't like the outcome of that meeting."

"Now, you be honest with me. How are you really doing?"

His hardness softened even more. "When they transferred me here, it became real, you know. As long as I was in Colorado I could pretend I was like the Unabomber, you know. A lifer." His winning smile appeared. "Actually, I am a lifer. Just a short-timer."

"Don't give me the same bullshit you gave the press about knowing when you're dying being a blessing. I know better."

"Yeah, well, everybody expects the heartless murderer to make a joke of life."

"Why give them what they expect?"

"Because I don't give a fuck anymore. Nobody gives a fuck about me, so why should I care?"

"I give a fuck."

"Right. I don't see you for a year. I leave phone messages, and it takes you days or weeks to call back."

"So, I make time from my work to be here, and you give me a ration of shit about it."

"Look, I want this to be over with."

She gave him her own smirk. "Tell your lawyers to stop the appeals."

That set him aback, and she watched the anger, frustration, and resignation play out.

"I can't let my family think I've given in. I wish sometimes, I'd have a heart attack or a stroke. I mean, why do you think I'm packing on the weight? Trying to kill myself is impossible when I'm watched twenty-four hours a day. You say you care, but if you did, you'd put me out of this hell."

"I couldn't do that before. Why do you think I could now?"

"You've killed before. Why not me?"

"I killed people who deserved it."

"I'm evil incarnate. The Kansas City bomber. The Monster in Human Skin. And I don't deserve it?"

"You and I know you were misled by someone who was evil incarnate."

"Liberal excuse-making."

"Look, do you think I came here to listen to you feel sorry for yourself?"

The defiance left him again. "I'm sorry. I get down sometimes."

"You're in prison. What do you expect?"

Red spots flared on his cheeks, a marker for his anger or other strong emotion.

"You remember that morning after Elijah beat you, I took you to that hotel in Kingman?"

How could she forget? She had put her gun to Carroll's chest but couldn't pull the trigger. If she had, neither of them would be here now, and a lot of people would still be alive.

"Yes, I remember."

"Sometimes I have this dream where we're there, and you do pull the trigger."

She closed her eyes for a moment and said, "I have the same dream."

"You could do it. You know how to find a way. Make it look like heart failure or something. You could do that."

"Don't ask me for that. Ask me for something I can give you."

"What I want is to be free, and the only way I'll be free is to die."

She had once told the people who would prosecute him that the worst punishment they could give him was to take away his liberty, that killing him would be his release. How prophetic.

"I told you before, another wrong won't make this right. Enough people have died."

"And I'll be the last, but what will I be in three more years, five more years, whenever the appeals are done, the appeals we all know I'm going to lose? I'll really be mad. I already feel myself slipping away sometimes. They won't let me read what I want to read. They won't let me have my music. They censor the news I get. I'm lost."

"You were lost before, when you listened to Elijah."

"Elijah gave me purpose."

"He sold you a bill of goods about being chosen, about your destiny. He was too much of a coward to do the deed himself, so he conned you into it. And don't fool yourself into thinking he'll fulfill any of those promises he made."

"Maybe he'll end up being the only person in my life I could rely on."

Mai laughed, shaking her head. "You don't get it, Jay. He put you here. Now you have to live with it, or die with it, as the case may be."

He gave her a knowing smile. "Prophet will move only when the time is right."

"Prophet is dead."

"No, he's in hiding somewhere."

"He was there with you, and he died there. That mysterious extra leg your lawyers tried to focus the jury on, that was all that was left of the Prophet of Patriot City. You want to know how I know that? I know the man who put a bullet between his eyes. Remember the gunshot we heard in the alley?"

"You're lying."

"No. That's the truth."

He processed the information for a while, then turned her logic on her. "So, you're all I have left. Are you going to let me down, too?"

"That's the problem, isn't it? Everyone let you down. The Army, the government, your mother, Elijah, me. Did you ever stop to think how many people you let down when you parked that bomb in front of a building and ran away? Jesus, take some responsibility for what you did before you die."

The spots of color on his cheeks deepened, matching her own anger.

Then, his face shifted into that soulless, unfeeling monster he had been on a day in April nearly six years before.

"You can leave now with a clear conscience," he said. His voice choked on the emotions he tried to hide. "You don't have to come back. Ever."

"You can't deny that fundamental thing, that basic act. I was there. You want to die easy, then live up to what you did."

"I will when you will."

"I have. It's done."

"Really? I don't see you sitting here waiting for your government to shove a needle in your leg." He stood up and walked to the door. "I'm ready to go back," he told the guards.

The guards came in, and two of them took him by the arms.

"Jay," Mai called to him.

"No!" He glanced at her over his shoulder. "Go ahead and let me down. Leave me alone."

"I made a promise. I'll keep it."

He had started to walk away, but he stopped and turned to her, his body still stiff with anger. She saw the relief on his face.

3

December 30, 1999
Lamar, Missouri

Twelve hours after she arrived in Washington, D.C., Mai was back in her aircraft headed for the state of Missouri, a place she was not fond of and had hoped never to see again. She glanced across the aisle at Munro. He had insisted he accompany her. She had tried every trick in the book, short of fucking him, to dissuade him. She had even appealed to his sense of duty, but he had extolled the capabilities of his second-in-command. Since he was in charge, he pointed out, it was incumbent upon him to follow the lead The Directorate had found.

"Besides," he said, "if this woman needs to be arrested, I'm the only one who can do that."

She gave in and, in truth, didn't mind the company on the flight.

Based on what Alexei had remembered, Directorate analysts had checked court records in Missouri and found a custody order allowing "Elijah Prophet" visitation rights with his daughter at her mother's home in Lamar. More digging showed that Patriot City funds had purchased the house, which had been deeded to the woman, free and clear. And, of course, both sources had the address.

With a county map from the car rental kiosk, Mai and Munro headed there from the small airport in Joplin. In case they would need it, Munro carried a warrant from a Federal judge in Washington.

Carlene Harper's ranch-style house was common in rural Missouri, its size and shape not much different from the abode it was a step-up from—a double-wide trailer. The house and yard were well-kept and surrounded by a six-foot high, chain-link fence, festooned with "No Trespassing" and "Beware of Dog" signs.

When Mai and Munro stepped from the car and approached the gate, they soon saw the reason for the latter sign. From behind the house, a beefy Rottweiler charged, teeth bared, a growl ululating from its throat. The dog launched itself at the fence, and Munro took an involuntary step back. Mai stood her ground.

"Easy, boy. Shh," she said.

The dog began a fierce barking, with an occasional snap at them from behind the fence.

"Yeah, that helped," Munro muttered.

"It was worth a try."

The front door opened, and the muzzle of a shotgun appeared. Munro's hand snaked under his jacket for his gun, but Mai stayed his arm.

"Ms. Harper?" she called out. She had dropped most of the English accent from her voice. "Could you call off the dog so we can talk?" The shotgun's muzzle swung from one of them to the other, and Mai felt Munro tense again. "Easy, Munro. A shotgun can't do us much harm from there."

Munro pulled from her grasp. "Carlene Harper! Federal agent! I have a warrant!"

"That won't ingratiate you to a Patriot City follower, Munro."

The door opened wider, and a woman in her late forties emerged, shotgun cradled in one arm. Her laughter reached them.

"Federal agent? I'm sure I'll piss my pants at that. Can't you Feds read? No trespassing."

"We need to ask you some questions," Munro said.

"Ask 'em."

"Could we come inside?"

"I'm not about to get Weavered. Ask 'em from there."

"Weavered?" Munro asked Mai.

"Randy Weaver in Idaho, when the FBI shot his wife."

Munro gave her a "are-you-nuts" expression and brought out his piece of paper. "I have a warrant," he shouted toward the house.

"Munro..." Mai said.

Harper's laughter reached them again. "Ya'll better get back in your car and get the hell outta here. If I shoot you and drag you inside, who do you think the local sheriff will believe? The Federal Government," she said with a sneer, "or a helpless single mother living alone trying to protect herself?"

"If we leave, more of us will be back," Munro said.

"And I'll be gone before your jackboots can get here."

Mai looked at Munro. "Let me try." She didn't wait for his permission, not that she would, and took a step closer to the fence. She ignored the renewed snarling from the dog.

"Ms. Harper, do you remember Sarai?"

Even from the distance, Mai could see the distaste on the woman's face. "How do you know about Sarai?"

"I know she had you kicked out of Patriot City, you and your daughter, Elijah's first born."

"What about the bitch?"

"I need to know her real name."

"Why?"

"To stop her from doing something she's planning."

Harper laughed. "Against the Feds? Then, I say, go Sister!"

"No, not the Feds. Innocent people, but she says she's doing it in Prophet's name. Does she have the right to that?"

"No! I was the first. I was Elijah's first, and she cast me out."

"That's right. Into the wilderness, as if you were the handmaiden, not she. Do you want history to remember her as the one who continued Prophet's legacy?"

Mai watched the wheels turn, and knew she'd succeeded when Carlene Harper nodded her head.

"Amelia Saint Clare. Now get outta here, or I'll use the remote on the gate and sic Adolph on you."

Mai's "Thank you, Ms. Harper" was delivered to the woman's back. The slam of the door set the dog off yet again.

Munro led the way back to the car, and once they were inside and headed away, Munro asked, "How do you know she's not inside calling Sarai right now and warning her?"

"Because Carlene Harper hates Sarai more than she hates the Feds."

"How do you know that?"

"Because I spent nearly three years immersed in their crap. I know." She took out her mobile phone and handed it to him. "Let's not waste any time. Amelia Saint Claire. Get your people started on tracking her down."

* * *

Another plane ride later, Munro led Mai Fisher back into his Mall-side command center. His second in command, a no-nonsense FBI agent in her forties, came up to him with a report.

"Vital records search showed us 153 Amelia Saint Claire's in the country. Only one in Idaho. That's where she was until six months ago."

"What happened six months ago?" Mai asked.

His 2IC looked to Munro for a nod before she answered. "She applied for unemployment benefits from a truck stop waitressing job and collected benefits for about eight weeks. Then nothing. She did, however, have a driver's license in Idaho."

The woman handed over an eight by ten blow-up of a typical license photo.

The woman in the picture was the poster child for sullen. Mousy blonde hair pulled up into a knot on the top of her head. No make-up. A nondescript face hard to spot in a crowd, and Mai searched in vain for some distinguishing mark.

The FBI agent continued her report. "She generally matches the description of a woman who has held up three banks, a gun shop, and a pawn shop on a line from Idaho heading east."

"How much money from the bank robberies?" Mai asked.

Again, the FBI agent sought Munro's permission. "Ten thousand from the first one. Seventy-five hundred and five thousand from the other two."

"What did she get from the gun store and pawn shop?"

"Shotguns, .45 caliber handguns, an Uzi." Mai canted an eyebrow at the latter weapon, which was supposed to be illegal to sell in the U.S. "From the shop owner's private collection."

"So, she's armed and financed," Mai said. "Where's her child?"

"With relatives in Idaho. They live in Aryan Nations."

"Why?" Munro asked. Mai looked at him and shrugged. "No, we're not using her child."

"No, we're not," Mai said. "Since it's your operation. Where was the last robbery and how long ago?"

"In Pittsburgh, Pennsylvania, three weeks ago," the FBI agent said.

"Do you have any surveillance on William Pierce's place in West Virginia?" Mai asked her.

"National Alliance? Only occasionally. Why?"

"Sometimes these lone wolves go to places where they know they can hide with impunity. Compounds, safe houses in a network Patriot City established."

"We can haul someone from National Alliance in and question him," the FBI agent offered.

"That'll do no good. They won't acknowledge she was there, and even if they did, they wouldn't know what she was up to. Leaderless resistance is something she knows well if she spent time in Aryan Nations."

"So, what do we do?" the FBI agent asked.

"Short of calling the whole thing off tomorrow, keep your eyes and ears open," came a man's voice from the direction of Munro's inner office.

Munro turned at the sound, but Mai didn't need to.

The FBI agent spoke up, "Sorry, Agent Munro, I didn't get a chance to tell you Mr. Bukharin arrived this morning. From the U.N. secretary-general's office."

Mai finally turned around and saw Alexei had dressed in a killer suit, and the enclosed space made him look taller than his full six-foot-two. She sometimes forgot how good looking he was—clear blue eyes surrounded by pale yellow lashes, gray, nearly white, hair brushing the collar of his jacket. The smile was sardonic and directed at her. Mai heard the FBI agent sigh and almost laughed.

"Munro, I believe you remember my husband, Alexei Bukharin," she said.

The FBI agent's disappointment at hearing the word "husband" was as acute as Munro's discomfort, but the two men shook hands, after Munro squared his shoulders. The handshake went on for a while, and the knuckles on both men's hands went white.

Alexei gave in first and released Munro's hand. "Excellent set-up here, Agent Munro."

"Thank you, Agent Bukharin."

"No longer Agent Bukharin. Just special representative now, but, please, call me Alexei. I'm only here in a semi-official capacity."

"Semi-official?"

Alexei walked to Mai's side and gave her a wink. "My wife faxed me a copy of the threatening letter you received. I was inside Patriot City, and I thought it best I at least be on hand as a resource."

Mai handed him the photo. "This is Amelia Saint Claire, aka Sarai."

Alexei took the picture and brought out his reading glasses. He perched the half-glasses on the end of his nose and studied the photo. "She was a few years younger when I was there, of course, and I only encountered her at mass meetings, but I recognize her."

"You obviously overheard the information we received," Mai said.

"About the robberies, yes." He gave her a smile to show her he was ignoring the tension in her tone. He looked at Munro. "How many officers will you have in and around the crowd?"

Munro looked to his second. "Brenda, what was the last count?"

"As of noon tomorrow, we will have nearly 7,500 police and other law enforcement officers on duty at the Main Street Millennium venue and along the Mall."

"You need to get the fax machines going," Alexei said. "Every officer needs a copy of that picture. Tell them she should be considered armed and extremely dangerous. She's been indoctrinated any law enforcement officer is an agent of a godless government. Tell them not to be fooled by her small stature. She thinks she's doing God's work. Do you have surveillance cameras around the Mall?"

"Yes," Mai said, but Munro and Brenda shifted in discomfort.

"Oh, don't worry Agent Munro, that secret is safe with me," Alexei said, and smiled in reassurance. "I'd like to be where I can see the monitors. I might be able to spot her. I'll need to be linked into your commo frequency so I can direct officers to her if I do."

Alexei's discerning eyes shifted from Munro to Brenda then to Mai.

"Is there some problem?"

"Agent Munro isn't quite accustomed to your take-charge demeanor, Alexei," Mai said. "Besides, you know how the Feds are when we show up."

"Agent Munro, I'm not here to usurp anyone's authority. I'm a resource, and a good one. That's all I'll be here. If you object to my being linked in on your communications, I don't have to be, but it would be beneficial. Any movement of assets, of course, would be your decision."

"Pardon my reticence, Mr. Bukharin, but I wasn't exactly expecting you to show up and offer your resources," Munro said.

"Munro, I'd like to speak with you privately," Mai said.

"What?"

"Outside with me, please," she said and left the command center.

When they were clear of the large tent, Mai turned on him. "Munro, do not treat Alexei as if he's washed up or a rival to you. He's neither."

"I don't know what you're talking about."

"Please. The two of you nearly arm-wrestled, and I was getting stuffy from all the testosterone. Alexei can help you. Let him do what he does best."

"I asked you here, not him."

"But he knows more about Patriot City than probably anyone in the country. This is the same attitude that fucked up Ruby Ridge and Waco, and we got Kansas City out of that. If you don't start being a professional about this, Alexei and I will go back to The Hague and leave you to find this particular needle in your haystack."

"Is that why he's here?"

"Partly."

"What's the other part?"

"I'm his partner. And his wife, who happens to be here with you."

"Wait, I thought you said you didn't tell him about what happened in Sligo."

"Of course I told him, Munro. He had a right to know, and you can't seem to grasp the fact I can lie with impunity to get people to do what I want. You need to give him the benefit of the doubt and use his knowledge where it can assure a successful and safe outcome tomorrow. Now, can we go do some work?"

When they re-entered the command center, Alexei had said something that left Brenda giggling like a teenager. She blushed when she saw her boss and excused herself, muttering something about a perimeter check.

Mai caught Alexei's eye and shook her head, but he gave her an air of utter innocence.

"So, are we working together?" Alexei asked Munro.

"Of course, Mr. Bukharin," Munro said. "Let's go in my office and work out a plan." Munro disappeared into the command center's innards.

"'Mr. Bukharin' still?"

"Probably because you're being as big a prick as he was," Mai said.

"Probably. You were upset when we spoke yesterday."

"Is that why you came?"

"I'm here because I know Patriot City, but, yes, that's why I came. I'm sorry I kept casually mentioning Karen. I consider it behind me, but I shouldn't have assumed it's behind us."

"You know, you have this uncanny knack for knowing when I'm completely pissed at you and apologizing before I ever get to make my points."

"All these years, and I've come to read you pretty well. Would you like for me to apologize to Agent Munro as well?"

"I'll leave that entirely up to you." She stepped closer to him, tipped up on her toes, and kissed him. "I'm glad you're here."

"I'm a bit jet-lagged, but I think if you took me home, I could make you even gladder."

"Later. After we plan." She headed for Munro's office.

"Obviously, we have some work to do on priorities," Alexei said, and followed her.

4

December 31, 1999
The National Mall

There was no refuge from the godless. Sin and corruption were everywhere, rolling off everyone like the stench of the pits of Hell.

Yahweh, my Creator, shield me from depravity. Strengthen my heart. Make my aim true.

She had to be careful here, where anyone could be an agent of ZOG—the Zionist Occupied Government. She couldn't pray in the open. They would fall on her and chastise her. Yahweh would forgive her for hiding her praying. He understood she needed to look other than what she was—his Messenger, his Instrument.

She walked among the crowds, holding in her disgust at the young women displaying themselves, men looking at them with open lust. A lesser person, one not emboldened by Yahweh, would have cringed from such an immersion in evil.

All the symbols of the godless Jew government surrounded her—monuments to nonbelievers, to Jews, to Freemasons. But she was strong. Nothing touched her.

Yet, whenever a young family passed her, the faces of the children made her yearn for her son. She ached for him. That parting had been the hardest, but Prophet's voice steeled her and reminded her she did this for her son, to make a better world for him. That was what Prophet had become a martyr for. That was what he whispered to her in her dreams.

Her commitment to what had to be done for Elijah and, through him, for Yahweh wouldn't waver. Her faith wouldn't allow that, but she could regret never seeing her son again. Her only solace she'd left him with Yahweh-fearing people who would raise him to be proud of his race, to plant his seed for his race as his father had, and to remember how brave and true his mother had been.

Still, Amelia Saint Claire would have liked to have held her son this morning, would have loved to hold her fine, Aryan grandsons in her arms. In assurance, Elijah's voice told her once she had completed Yahweh's work, she would join him in Heaven to look down upon and bless their son, their future grandchildren.

That she would wake from death in Paradise at Elijah's side, she was certain. Her faith allowed no questioning of that. She had been Elijah's faithful servant and, thus, Yahweh's. She had borne Elijah's son, endured the break-up of Patriot City, an uncertain future after Elijah's death. There had been no body to weep over, but she knew. He would have returned to her, his true wife, had he been able. But he was with her still—his beautiful, soothing, inspiring voice and his form itself, like an angel, shining his light on her.

At first she had resisted his calling. After all, bloodletting was the Holy Cause and work of Aryan Warriors, who were all men. An Aryan woman's sole and holiest duty was to accept the warrior's seed, bear the next generation of warriors, and teach the daughters their godly duties.

Elijah had persisted, rejecting her protestations, and the more she prayed on it, the more she became convinced Elijah had called her to do Yahweh's work.

Amelia, always called Sarai by her beloved, had prevailed upon the warriors at Aryan Nations to train her, to teach her how to kill. Elijah told her to be free with her affections, so she could learn and be worthy of her god-given task. An apt pupil, she had earned the men's praise and endured their lust, imagining herself again in Elijah's bed. She knew she had his forgiveness. He had told her to do whatever she needed to be ready and able.

Soon, she was accurate and comfortable with a variety of weapons. She waited and practiced until Elijah told her where and when, and when he did, she marveled again at his genius, at his sense of timing. Even in death, he understood symbolism.

What better way to herald the End Times than wreaking Yahweh's wrath during the celebration of the false millennium?

Elijah had taught a war between the races would accelerate the End Times and bring Yahweh's Kingdom to earth. She—a proud white woman—now walked among the godless, untainted by their filth. She would show them Yahweh's wrath with the race-mixers, the miscegenation. They and their mongrels would be the only sacrifice.

The crowd and its ebullience threatened to overwhelm her, and she longed for the quiet beauty of the mountains in the Sawtooth Range and the long walks she took with her son, teaching him, telling him of his father in heaven and the destiny that awaited him when he was older. She would miss that, but she couldn't dwell on it.

Focus, came Elijah's voice, so clear and close she thought he must be at her side. Her eyes sought and found her first target. Nausea rolled in her stomach at the sight of a beautiful Aryan woman pressed against a nigger. Sarai wanted to keen and beat her breast. How could this flower of white womanhood defile her purity this way?

No, Elijah said. You cannot think of this whore as pure. You lie down with filth, you become filth.

There was no child with them, but Elijah told her the woman's womb, where only Aryan warriors should grow, already carried a mongrel monster. Later, Sarai would weep for the lost womb that would not bear proud, white children. Now, she gave herself over to her holy cause.

Sarai touched the warmth of the sawed-off shotgun through her long coat and set forth, murmuring prayers she knew Elijah heard.

* * *

An unseasonably warm last day of December made the crowd more enthusiastic. The event was booze-free since it was on Federal land, so politeness ruled the evening. A true family affair, adults strolled arm in arm, surrounded by their broods of all ages. The backdrop of the Washington, D.C., monuments made it all so quintessentially American, and Mai Fisher restrained her cynicism.

The entertainment had begun, but she paid little attention to it as she moved among the crowds, eyes seeking a single face. The excitement was contagious, and she gave a thought to chucking this all and getting Alexei down here to enjoy it. That would be better than walking among the boisterous people looking for America's dark side.

Long ago, she'd learned to tune out the constant streams of tactical exchanges on her radio and pick out only what she needed. She did double duty tonight, though. One ear bud plugged her into the main frequency for the event's security. The other was a direct line to Alexei and only Alexei, in case she needed to indulge in something Munro didn't need to know about.

Alexei spoke only when he needed, as was always the case, but even after working for the most part on her own for the past two years, she took comfort from the calm, modulated voice.

Of course, she'd never tell him that. They were together, and that was all that mattered.

No, their personal happiness wasn't all that mattered. Alexei wanted what he thought was a normal life, but that was never theirs to embrace and would never be. There was injustice in the world—there always would be—and never had she been more alive than when she fought that and won. No amount of domesticity would ever substitute for making a difference.

Such thoughts were a distraction, and she filed them away. Their relationship had always evolved, had never been static, and their life was different now. That was where she needed to find fulfillment.

She had to.

* * *

Alexei rubbed first one tired eye, then the other so he could keep at least one of them fixed on the images transmitted from the numerous surveillance cameras around the Mall. Munro paced behind him, and Alexei could hear his measured voice encouraging his forces.

Munro sweated. Alexei was cool. Munro was tense, Alexei relaxed. A contrast in styles, he supposed, but Munro was a divorced, repressed Catholic. Alexei had shown Mai last night and this morning he was far from that.

In truth, his ego didn't let him see Munro as a rival, though he was another of Mai's inadvertent conquests. Some men wanted to be her willing slaves while others took a while to get there. The remainder couldn't stand her on sight but wanted to fuck her anyway, and she never understood, truthfully, why any of it happened. With a smile he wondered which group he fell in but decided it was an exclusive group of one who loved and respected her more than his own life.

He refocused on the monitors, where he'd spent hours searching for a glimpse of Amelia Saint Claire. Spotting her was unlikely at best. More like impossible. A last-minute call to local jurisdictions had added another 2,000 officers to Munro's task force, and Alexei could only hope that would put her off.

Alexei recalled the words from her threatening letter: "erase the scourge of miscegenation" from the "capital of Yahweh's greatest nation." She wouldn't be put off by much, short of a direct communication from God to cease and desist.

Munro took his optimism from the increased police presence, but he hadn't been in Patriot City. Munro hadn't been subjected to a daily stream of intolerance and racism, nationalism, neo-Nazi philosophy, and Christian Identity.

The months in Patriot City had left a mark on Alexei's wounded psyche and prolonged his re-integration into his usual life. His infidelity while there hadn't helped that either, and Mai had made certain he didn't forget that. He didn't blame her, but it was another reason to despise Amelia Saint Claire and her ilk. Without her threat, he wouldn't be sitting here remembering all the things he hated about Patriot City.

Elijah's racist vitriol he called sermons.

Alexei's own role while undercover in teaching people how to kill.

Pretending to believe in Elijah's garbage, spewed in Patriot City's publications and videos.

Finding solace in an incredibly brave woman, a Jewish ATF agent who had been undercover in Patriot City two years longer than he.

Karen Wolfe had survived Patriot City, their escape from it, and a bounty placed on them by Elijah. She died months later in Kansas City, the victim of a coward's bomb.

That angered him, still angered him, and it was something he couldn't share with Mai. She would interpret his anger as feelings for Karen. Of course he had cared about Karen, though not in the way he cared for Mai. Karen had been a convenience, much as he considered Mai in the early years of their relationship. He had used Karen and disappointed everyone.

Alexei, he told himself, you are getting old, dwelling on depressing events from your past. His Russian side took over—what's past is past. Look to the future. He'd seen Mai's eyes alight with the thrill she got from this aspect of their work, and the future he'd seen falling into place now wasn't so certain.

Before he could wallow, a figure on one of the monitors caught his eyes, and he felt a familiar surge of adrenaline. Without alerting Munro, Alexei typed a command on the keyboard in front of him that would isolate that particular camera. Typing some more, he zoomed in on a woman strolling through the crowd. The woman's image wasn't face-on, but it was enough to make a good guess. The nose was the same as the driver's license photo, as was the ear he saw. Ear patterns were almost as distinctive as fingerprints. He zoomed in some more and saw it was Amelia Saint Claire.

He'd seen faces like hers in Patriot City, distorted with hate and loathing. He studied her eyes. Hers were fastened on someone ahead and to her left, and he zoomed the camera out to see if he could spot what she saw. When he did, he switched his radio to Mai's discrete frequency.

"Mai, sitrep."

A few seconds went by as she must have made the switch off Munro's frequency, and she replied, "I'm about midway on the south side of the Reflecting Pool. Do you see her?"

He backed the camera off some more. "Wave," he said. He saw a hand go up in the vicinity where she said she was and compared it to Saint Clair's position. "She is directly across the Reflecting Pool from you, headed toward the Washington Monument. She's following an interracial couple. She's wearing a long, denim coat, unbuttoned."

"Can you make out a weapon?"

"No, but given the length of the coat, anything from an AK-47 to a sawed-off shotgun."

"Do you want me to handle this?"

He heard her elevated breathing. "Yes. Do you want back-up?"

"Let's not spook her, but I'll let you know."

"Fine, but I reserve the right to send the cavalry."

"My trust is in your impeccable judgement. I'm going radio silence until I spot her, but keep updating me."

"Roger." Alexei covered his mic and called to Munro.

Munro came and stood at his shoulder. "Damn," he said, eyes on the monitor. "You found her."

"Mai is intercepting."

"Only Mai?"

Alexei looked up at Munro. "Look at that crowd. Too much potential for collateral damage."

"The Secret Service isn't the FBI, Mr. Bukharin. Our cowboy quotient is low."

That got a smile from Alexei, but it was an apt description. "Can you alert only your own agents?"

"You're not the only one with a discrete frequency. Give me the particulars."

Munro took little time to alert his men and get them moving through the crowd. Mai's voice sounded in Alexei's ear.

"I have her in sight."

"Approach with caution."

"Of course. I'm converging. I'm going to pass her and come up behind."

Alexei manipulated the next camera in the sequence along the Mall. "Okay, I see you." He murmured something to her in Russian and smiled when he heard her laugh.

Munro stared at him.

"It's nothing, Agent Munro. A little superstition of mine. I always tell her I love her when she's about to go into action."

Munro shook his head. "The two of you have to be the oddest married people I've ever met, and I had an odd marriage."

"Odd?" Alexei considered the description. "I prefer unique."

* * *

Mai slipped past Sarai without betraying she knew who the woman was. An amateur, Sarai was so focused on her potential target, nothing else from her surroundings touched her. A few strides past her, Mai turned and crept back to an arm's length away. Mai took in the crowd, in case Sarai had an unknown accomplice.

One of the Jumbo-Trons showed the stage entertainment nearing its conclusion.

Mai checked her watch. Seven minutes until midnight. A roar would go up from the crowd at the end of the countdown, one loud enough to cover the sound of gunfire.

Mai could wait for the cover of sound, slip up to Amelia Saint Claire, put the Beretta against the woman's back, and pull the trigger. Everything would be over, and who would miss a bigot?

Her child, for one. Alexei wouldn't hesitate, but he'd also want this woman in an interrogation room. Mai took a breath to ease the effect of the adrenaline and murmured into her mic.

"Sitrep?"

"Four agents converging," Alexei said. "ETA eight minutes."

"I can't wait for them."

She turned off both her radios and reached inside her own coat, brought out the Beretta, and held it down by her thigh within a fold of the coat. She let the crowd bear her closer to Saint Claire. When it jostled her against the woman's back, Mai gripped the woman's collar and pushed the Beretta against her spine.

"Move, and you're dead," Mai said.

Sarai turned her head. "You smell like ZOG. ZOG cannot stop me. I have Yahweh in my heart, and Elijah the Prophet by my side."

"Elijah is in hell. You and I, we're moving toward Constitution Avenue, where some more agents of ZOG will take you into custody. Reach for your weapon, and I'll shoot you right here."

* * *

Alexei wasn't surprised when she didn't respond to his radio calls. He pulled his mic off and tossed it on the desk, his eyes fixed on the monitor as he watched her move in on Saint Claire.

"What the hell is she doing? Why isn't she waiting for my men?" Munro asked.

"She's doing what she does best. Improvising." Alexei stood and checked how much ammunition he had for his Taurus PT111. "I'm going to help her. You're welcome to come, but where she's concerned, it's my show."

Munro called someone over to track Mai and her captive on the monitor.

"You tell us every movement," Munro said to the agent. He handed Alexei an MP-5, twin to his own, and said, "Let's go."

* * *

Amelia Saint Claire resisted Mai as much as she could, but Mai kept them on a steady march through the crowd toward Constitution Avenue.

"You keep me from God's work," Saint Claire said.

"God can take it up with me later. If you don't move faster, I'll…"

Saint Claire halted abruptly, throwing Mai off-balance enough for the woman to elbow her ribs and kick her shin. Mai lost her hold, and Saint Claire began to run, pushing people aside as she did.

"Fuck!" Mai said and turned her radio back on as she ignored her throbbing shin and ran after the woman. "She got away. She's headed north. She just crossed Constitution…" She glanced at the street sign as she ran past. "…and Eighteenth."

"Munro and I are maybe two minutes behind you," Alexei said. "She'll soon be out of camera range. Keep giving me position reports."

Mai was as rude to people as Sarai, but they were too intent on the imminent countdown to react. On the other side of Constitution Avenue, the crowd had thinned and gave way when they saw her running, gun out. Sarai turned corners without hesitation, so she must have studied a map of D.C. well. Mai suspected she was headed toward a getaway car parked outside the tow-zone for the event. Mai broadcast each turn and barely heard Alexei's acknowledgements.

Then, her Irish luck decided to make a visit. Sarai turned into what she must have thought was an alley and found herself in a dead-end courtyard of an office building. Mai brought the Beretta up, gripped in both hands to steady it after her all-out run, and went in after her.

Sarai turned in a circle, twice, her eyes seeking a way out, but Mai grinned, knowing she was trapped. Sarai stared at Mai and smiled.

"The Lord is my shepherd," Sarai began as she pulled a sawed-off shotgun from beneath her coat.

"No! Drop it!" Mai said. "Put it down! Now!"

"I shall not want. He maketh me to lie down in green pastures."

"Drop it or I shoot." Their weapons pointed at each other, both women panted. "Sarai, you have no way out."

"Yahweh will find a way. He always does. He leadeth me beside still waters. He restoreth my soul."

"Well, he better start parting the Red Sea or something right now, because a lot of my friends are on the way."

Sarai laughed, and it echoed around the courtyard. "You can kill me, but Elijah lives on. Forever. He lives in me. In every white warrior on earth. He prepareth me a table in the presence of mine enemies."

Sarai's finger tensed on the shotgun's trigger, and Mai dived behind a large planter as the shot gouged a chunk of concrete from it. Mai crouched and edged to the side of the planter and got off two shots, but Sarai had her own concrete planter to hide behind, too.

"Crap," Mai muttered and checked her ammunition. Two more full magazines besides the one in the Beretta, but she had no idea how many shells Sarai had.

A shotgun blast hit the top of the planter, sending dirt and bits of concrete over Mai's shoulders. Mai sent two more shots in Sarai's direction to keep her from charging. She keyed her mic and gave Alexei her position and situation.

"We're on our way. Thirty seconds," Alexei said, his voice calm, cool, as always.

"Careful. There's only one way in, and she's got it in her sights."

"Get ready for a flash-bang."

"Ah, shite."

The Secret Service followed the flash-bang grenade with tear gas, and Mai thought it a secret plot to deafen and blind her. She couldn't quibble with the results.

Amelia Saint Claire was in custody and screaming her prayers to a god that didn't exist. As they shoved the failed assassin in a car, Alexei handed Mai a handkerchief, and the fireworks on the Mall exploded to celebrate an event that was a year away.

5

January 1, 2000
Washington, D.C.

Mai rinsed her eyes one more time and peered at herself in the bathroom mirror. Two days of scant sleep and a good dose of tear gas, and she looked as if she'd been on a week-long drunk. How attractive.

She pulled some paper towels from the dispenser and blew her nose, which ran as much as her eyes. Some cold water addressed the swelling somewhat, and she washed her hands and left the basement ladies room of the BATF building.

The BATF building had been closest to the scene of Saint Claire's arrest, and Mai wondered if they'd put the interrogation rooms in the basement to confirm a stereotype or were in ignorance of it.

To the BATF's delight, Saint Claire had emphasized she didn't want an attorney, but Mai knew by the time she got before a judge, Saint Claire would have one whether she wanted it or not. Until then, she was spilling her guts, and it had started in the car on the drive here.

While Sarai spoke of Elijah as a living person who shared her bed and guided her hand, Alexei's jaw had clenched tighter and tighter. Yet, there he was, in the observation room listening to more of the woman's drivel. Even from down the hallway, she could see the tension in his shoulders and neck.

She stopped, still several meters away and leaned against the wall. Mai had known exactly what the outcome was going to be tonight. As they had for so many years, she and Alexei had planned an operation and executed it as planned and without casualties. The result, for them, had never been in doubt.

And, God, she had missed it.

When the adrenaline hit her bloodstream on her first sight of Sarai, Mai had felt as invincible as cocaine used to make her. She had taken the situation into her hands and managed it, with no lives lost, and she had made a difference.

That was the point. She and Alexei had always made a difference. In a few days, they'd go back to The Hague, where she would make out personnel schedules, spot-check security procedures, and fill out endless paperwork.

Had Munro not requested her for this, she would never have known how meaningless her job at The Hague was. She had taken it for the wrong reason—to make someone else happy—but now she knew she couldn't go back.

The tight knot in her chest loosened, and she finished her walk to the observation room.

Her hand touched Alexei's arm, and she felt him lean against her. "Are you all right?" she asked.

"I've been running that day through my head," he said.

No need for him to say which one. That was a failure they both shared.

"I shot Elijah between the eyes. I know he's dead, but to hear her talk about him as if he's here…" He shook his head.

"She's delusional—either for real, or she's setting up a good defense. Or he really is the second coming, and we're all in trouble."

He laughed, and his arm slid around her shoulders. "You must have driven the nuns insane," he said.

"Between my blasphemy and my, let's see, what did Sister Ignatious call it? Oh, yes, my 'heathen proclivities,' I pretty much kept them on their toes."

Alexei looked at her with that expression that both thrilled and discomfited her, where his feelings were out for all the world to see.

"You look like you've been crying for a week. Sorry about the tear gas," he said.

"And my ears are still ringing. Do they need us anymore, or can we go home?"

"Home would be good. I put a bottle of Dom Perignon to chill for today."

Somehow, she managed a convincing smile, but she wondered how she could tell him her decision. The only way to preclude the inevitable argument would be to leave while he slept off the sex.

"It's 0600, Alexei. A little early for champagne."

"Ah, it's never too early for good champagne."

"I see they raised one hedonist in the Ukrainian SSR. I'll go tell Munro we're leaving. Where did we leave the car, anyway?"

"In the DoJ's parking garage. You want me to wait for you, or meet me there?"

"I'll meet you there."

He pressed a kiss to her temple. "No protracted goodbyes for Agent Munro," he said. "No need to give him hope."

Mai remembered Munro's kiss in a safe house in Sligo had sent her back to Alexei and to The Hague. Not this time.

* * *

Munro stood with several agents and watched the interrogation of Amelia Saint Claire. His face was stern, his arms folded over his chest.

"Munro?"

He turned to her with a smile and approached her. "You look a little better," he said, after studying her face. "Kinda weepy and vulnerable, though."

"Ah, now we see you like women who want to be rescued."

"Only in my fantasies."

"Confess those to Father, do you?"

"I don't recall a Commandment about fantasies."

They laughed together, as if they were old and dear friends; then, the silence of strangers lay between them.

"I wanted to let you know, since we're of no further use to you, Alexei and I are headed home."

"Back to the Netherlands?"

Her hesitation was prolonged enough for him to notice.

"You *are* going back to the Netherlands, aren't you?"

"We'll spend a few days here, celebrate the New Year and all that. Look, I'll send you the information on my security business. Give it some thought. Serious thought."

"You're not going back to The Hague," he said.

Mai laid a hand on his cheek. "Happy New Year, Munro," she said and walked away.

The dawn's light slipped between the buildings and gave the city a beauty Mai had seldom appreciated. She shouldn't feel as optimistic, as excited as she was. She had to push that down so she could go to the home she and Alexei had built and lie to him long enough to make a clean getaway.

She would go back to Europe, and, even if it wouldn't be with him, she could do the work he taught her. She would leave him no choice but to be proud of the work, though he might hate her for leaving.

No, Alexei would never hate her, even though she'd disappointed him before.

There was a world to save, peace to make, and justice to be served, and she would be a part of it.

Y2K wasn't going to be so bad, after all.

THE END

ABOUT THE AUTHOR

P. A. Duncan is a retired bureaucrat but one with an overactive imagination—at least that's what everyone has told her since she first started making up stories in elementary school, prompted by her weekly list of spelling words. A commercial pilot and former FAA safety official, she lives and writes in the Shenandoah Valley of Virginia. A graduate of Madison College (now James Madison University), she has degrees in history and political science. Her love of politics continues to this day.

She is an officer on the Board of Governors of the Virginia Writers Club, one of the oldest writer organizations in the country.

Her fiction has appeared in numerous literary journals and anthologies. When not writing, editing, reading, reviewing books, singing in a UU choir, watching the Yankees, or cheering on Dale Earnhardt, Jr., she delights in spoiling her grandchildren.

SOCIAL MEDIA

Twitter: @unspywriter
Facebook Author Page: https://www.facebook.com/unspywriter/
Blog: www.unexpectedpaths.com
Instagram: paduncan1
Amazon Author Page: http://bit.ly/PADuncan (links to all published work)

ALSO BY THE AUTHOR

Short Story and Flash Fiction Collections

Rarely Well-Behaved, 2000 (out of print)
Blood Vengeance, 2012
Fences and Other Stories, 2012
Spy Flash, 2012
The Better Spy, 2015 (a novel in stories)
Spy Flash II, coming later in 2016

Novellas

My Noble Enemy, 2015
The Yellow Scarf, 2015

Novels

A War of Deception, coming in 2017

Short Story Singles*

"Spymaster," 2016
"Blood Cover," 2016
"Best Served Cold," 2016
"Brave New World," 2016

*compiled in *Spy Flash II*

Made in the USA
Charleston, SC
05 December 2016